DOCTOR WHO
AND THE
DAY OF THE DALEKS

THE CHANGING FACE OF DOCTOR WHO
The cover illustration and others contained within this book
portray the third DOCTOR WHO whose physical appearance
was altered by the Time Lords when they banished him to
the planet Earth in the Twentieth Century.

Also available from BBC Books:

DOCTOR WHO AND THE DALEKS
David Whitaker

DOCTOR WHO AND THE CRUSADERS
David Whitaker

DOCTOR WHO AND THE CYBERMEN
Gerry Davis

DOCTOR WHO AND THE ABOMINABLE SNOWMEN
Terrance Dicks

DOCTOR WHO AND THE AUTON INVASION
Terrance Dicks

DOCTOR WHO AND THE CAVE MONSTERS
Malcolm Hulke

DOCTOR WHO AND THE TENTH PLANET
Gerry Davis

DOCTOR WHO AND THE ICE WARRIORS
Brian Hayles

DOCTOR WHO – THE THREE DOCTORS
Terrance Dicks

DOCTOR WHO AND THE ARK IN SPACE
Ian Marter

DOCTOR WHO AND THE LOCH NESS MONSTER
Terrance Dicks

DOCTOR WHO
AND THE
DAY OF THE DALEKS

Based on the BBC television serial *Day of the Daleks* by Louis Marks by arrangement with the BBC

TERRANCE DICKS

Introduction by
GARY RUSSELL

Illustrated by
Chris Achilleos

BOOKS

1 3 5 7 9 10 8 6 4 2

Published in 2012 by BBC Books, an imprint of Ebury Publishing
A Random House Group Company
First published in 1974 by Universal-Tandem Publishing Co. Ltd.

Novelisation copyright © Terrance Dicks 1974
Original script © Louis Marks 1972
Illustrations © Chris Achilleos 1974
Introduction © Gary Russell 2012
The Changing Face of Doctor Who and About the Authors © Justin Richards 2012
Between the Lines © Steve Tribe 2012
Daleks created by Terry Nation

The Random House Group Limited Reg. No. 954009

Addresses for companies within the Random House Group can be found at
www.randomhouse.co.uk

A CIP catalogue record for this book is available from the British Library.

ISBN 978 1 849 90477 3

The Random House Group Limited supports The Forest Stewardship Council (FSC®), the
leading international forest certification organisation. Our books carrying the FSC label are
printed on FSC® certified paper. FSC is the only forest certification scheme endorsed by the
leading environmental organisations, including Greenpeace. Our paper procurement policy can
be found at www.randomhouse.co.uk/environment

Editorial director: Albert DePetrillo
Editorial manager: Nicholas Payne
Series consultant: Justin Richards
Project editor: Steve Tribe
Proofreader: Kari Speers
Cover design: Lee Binding © Woodlands Books Ltd, 2012
Cover illustration: Chris Achilleos
Production: Rebecca Jones

Printed and bound in Great Britain by Clays Ltd, St Ives PLC

To buy books by your favourite authors and register for offers,
visit www.randomhouse.co.uk

Contents

INTRODUCTION
BY
Gary Russell

So it's Easter 1974, and I'm not at school. Cos it's the holidays, by the way, not because I'm some terrible truculent truant (tempting as that was sometimes – I really didn't get on with 'school' as a concept). Anyway, unlike many of my contemporaries who remember buying their first *Doctor Who* novels from WH Smith or John Menzies back in the 1970s, for me it was Woolworth's. Not because they were especially famous for their literary sections but because their pick 'n' mix selection was too amazing not to stand and stare at and frantically dig out ten new pence (it had a lion grinning like a loon on one side and the Queen on the other – bigger than modern ones, it felt hefty and worth something to a 10-year-old) and indulge in these long, thin, brown and yellow stripy sweets that smelled of banana and tasted of enough sugar you could go through a mouthful of teeth in a day! I had in my hands three shiny ten-pee bits – that bought a lot of pick 'n' mix in 1974.

But then I was distracted – Maidenhead's Woolworth's conveniently placed the pick 'n' mix on a central freestanding bench right next to two tall racks of paperbacks. Now these tended to be a bit like airport books: a few of the latest bestsellers by Frederick Forsyth, a handful of Mills and Boon and, at the top, the latest by Xaviera Hollander, whose books I never understood but the covers were… eye-catching.

They also had a small cluster of SF books, about six usually, one of which was always a copy of *Star Trek 4* by James Blish. Always. I'm pretty sure I read that book a chapter a week in Woolworth's, it was there, unloved and unbought, that long. But this particular Easter afternoon, there were five books the like of which I had never seen before. They were *Doctor Who* books with marvellous colourful covers but with the Doctor drawn in black and white. And they were 30p each.

Banana sweets (yummy)? *Doctor Who* in book form. A book. About *Doctor Who*? No contest – except then it was which book to buy? I mean, I could easily discount the three with the old man from the past – yeah, I'd read about William Hartnell's Doctor in the *Radio Times Tenth Anniversary Special*, but two of these featured the proper Doctor. My Doctor. Jon Pertwee.

The Doomsday Weapon – not heard of that one. But this one, *Day of the Daleks* – oh, that was a title I knew.

And so that was my purchase that day.

I had read it by the time I went to sleep that night. I read it again the next day. I read it a lot of times that holiday, swapping days with reading *The Doomsday Weapon* (oh yes, pleas, beggings, tantrums and a pocket-money advance eventually secured that one the Monday afterwards).

And I was captivated because, although it had been only two years since 'Day of the Daleks' had been broadcast on telly, to a 10-year-old that was a lifetime away. I recalled nothing of it except the Controller getting exterminated. (I'd even written to *Ask Aspel*, asking them to show that clip when Jon Pertwee was a guest. They didn't. Bah – their loss.) Suddenly it was coming back to life before me and I fell in love, not just with *Doctor Who* books (a lifelong obsession ever since) but with words. With words conjured by Terrance Dicks. I confused him with Charles Dickens once at school – frankly I know which one I reckoned told better stories. He and Malcolm Hulke (who wrote *The Doomsday Weapon*) made me want to be a writer. Full stop. No amount of Blyton, Kipling, Uttley and every other writer's work I had devoured prior to this experience, held a candle to Dicks and Hulke. Oh sure, those other writers were good, but these two? They were genii.

Day of the Daleks also had pictures in it. Normally, at 10, I'd've pooh-poohed a book with pictures but these were amazing. An Ogron being knocked out by Jo (looking more like someone who'd stuck a wet finger in a socket than Jo to be honest), or Shura with his bomb, or (my favourite) Austerly House exploding at the end. And then on page 42 (p.44 in this new edition), that peculiar picture of Jo and the Doctor in front of the fireplace. Years later, I realised the reason it didn't look like Jo was because it's actually based on a photo of Jane Leeson from 'Colony in Space' – she turns up again on page 54 (p.59 here), this time pretending to be Anat.

All these little things contributed to this book being a treasure – and it's still treasured today. I'm looking at it now; that 30p copy I bought in Woolies is still here (unlike Woolies). Battered, creased but loved. Beside it sits a later Target edition. And the American one with a UNIT spaceship on it (I wonder why). And completing my *Day of the Daleks* obsession are *A Mudanca da Historia*, *O Dia dos Daleks*, *De Dag van de Daleks*, *Ve Dalek Baskini*, *Dzien Dalekow* and a Japanese one, *Darek Zoku no gyakushuu*, which is also full of wonderful pictures, drawn by someone who has clearly never seen an episode of *Doctor Who* in his life and presumably based the Daleks, Ogrons and Jo's fashion sense solely on Terrance's descriptions.

Day of the Daleks wasn't the first Target novel to be released, but it was *my* first. And like so many things in life, you always remember, cherish and love the first one that little bit more than is truly healthy.

It was also the first time I read and absorbed that fantastic Gerard Garrett quote on the back – '*Doctor Who*, the children's own programme which adults adore...' At 10 years old, I considered myself the adult in that scenario and thought it summed up why *Doctor Who* was the best TV show in history. At nearly 50, I still do...

The Changing Face of Doctor Who

The Third Doctor

This *Doctor Who* novel features the third incarnation of the Doctor, whose appearance was altered by his own people, the Time Lords, when they exiled him to Earth. This was his punishment for daring to steal a TARDIS, leave his home world and interfere in the affairs of other life forms. The Time Lords sentenced the Doctor to exile on twentieth-century Earth. The secrets of the TARDIS were taken from him and his appearance was changed.

While on Earth the Doctor formed an alliance and friendship with Brigadier Lethbridge-Stewart, head of the British branch of UNIT. Working as UNIT's Scientific Adviser, the Doctor helps the organisation to deal with all manner of threats to humanity in return for facilities to try to repair the TARDIS, and a sporty, yellow Edwardian-style car he calls Bessie.

UNIT

UNIT in the United Kingdom is under the command of the ever-practical and down-to-earth Brigadier Lethbridge-Stewart. He first met the Second Doctor, and fought with him against the Yeti and the Cybermen. UNIT is a military organisation, with its headquarters in Geneva but personnel seconded from the armed forces of each host nation. The remit of UNIT is rather vague but, according to the Brigadier, it deals with 'the odd, the unexplained. Anything on Earth, or even beyond...'

From mad scientists to alien invasions, from revived prehistoric civilisations to dinosaurs rampaging through London, UNIT has its work cut out.

Jo Grant

Jo Grant is an unlikely UNIT agent. Having been foisted on the Brigadier against his will at the insistence of her uncle – a high-ranking official in the UN – the Brigadier hits on the idea of assigning Jo to be the Doctor's assistant.

Jo tells the Doctor that she is a fully qualified agent, but – since she also tells him she took an A level in General Science, only to point out later 'I didn't say I passed' – this may be an exaggeration. But Jo's abilities in escapology and her enthusiasm are never in doubt. Very quickly, the Doctor and the Brigadier come to realise what an asset she really is.

But in an organisation as professional and disciplined as UNIT, Jo – like the Doctor – will always stand out as an individual who is not afraid to speak her mind and follow her own instincts.

1

Terror in the Twenty-Second Century

Moni sat up and looked around cautiously. The enormous dormitory was packed with sleeping forms, dragged into total exhaustion by hours of brutal physical toil. One or two murmured and twisted and cursed in their sleep. A man screamed, 'No, no, please don't...' and then his voice tailed off into the mutterings of a nightmare. Moni saw that it was Soran. He had been beaten by the guards that morning for failing to meet his work-norm. Soran was weakening daily. He wouldn't last much longer.

Somehow the incident seemed to give Moni courage. It was for Soran that he was fighting. Soran and thousands like him who would die in the work camps from brutal beatings, or worn out after years of grinding labour, unless... unless... Moni threw back the coarse blankets and swung his feet to the floor. There was nothing unusual in his being fully dressed. The dormitories weren't heated and most of his fellows slept fully clothed against the night cold. Vaguely Moni remembered having heard of a time when men had special clothes to sleep in – called py-something or other. His mind could scarcely imagine such luxury.

Moni fished his boots from beneath his pillow. He'd put

them there automatically the night before. The boots were made of new strong plastic, and in the work camps nothing valuable was safe unless it was within touching distance. Tucking the boots under his arm Moni moved silently across the room towards the door. His bare feet made no sound on the rough concrete floor.

Once in the compound, he paused in a patch of shadow to pull on the boots then crept silently along the edge of the outer wall. Taking off his tunic Moni uncoiled a thin plastic rope from round his waist. He took the crude grappling hook from his pocket, tied it to the rope and swung the grappling hook at the row of spikes on top of the wall. It fell short and landed back at Moni's feet with a metallic scrape. Moni froze in terror. He glanced towards the doorway of the guard's quarters. Surely they must have heard. But there came only the rumble of guttural inhuman speech. The compound was supposed to be patrolled at all times, but the guards were careless and idle. On cold nights like this they kept to their quarters, huddling round the roaring fires in the iron braziers, stuffing down slabs of coarse grey food that their masters provided.

Moni hurled the grapple again, and this time his luck was in. It caught firmly on the spikes and, after testing it with a tug, Moni climbed quickly up the rope, his tunic between his teeth. Once on top of the wall it would make a rough pad to protect him from the spikes. Awkwardly he bestrode the wall, pulling the rope up beside him, and freeing the grappling hook. He lowered the rope to the other side of the wall, dropped his tunic after it, and then jumped down, landing with a thud that jolted the breath out of him. Quickly he put on his tunic, and hid rope and grappling iron beneath it. He set off swiftly down the endless concrete road through the rubble.

Moni had covered several miles before his luck ran out. He was just turning the corner of one of the many ruined buildings when an enormous hairy hand reached out from the darkness and plucked him off his feet. The hand slammed him against the remains of a brick wall, making him gasp out loud. Moni flinched, as a burning brand was thrust uncomfortably close to his face, and as his eyes became accustomed to the light he could just begin to pick out the hulking shape of the creature that had captured him. Nearby was a small campfire with other giant forms huddled round it. Moni cursed his luck. He had run into one of the roving patrols, camping out in the ruins. From the campfire, a guttural voice said, 'Bring!' Moni's captor shambled back towards the fire, dragging Moni after him like a rag doll. Moni let himself hang limp, making no attempt to resist. He had no wish to be torn to pieces. Against human beings he might have stood a chance, but these guards were not human: these were Ogrons.

Thrown sprawling at the feet of the patrol, Moni looked up at the hulking shapes looming over him in the firelight. Often as he had seen them before, the Ogrons never failed to terrify him. Creatures somewhere between gorilla and man, they stood almost seven feet in height with bowed legs, massive chests and long powerful arms that hung almost to the ground. Their faces were perhaps the most awful thing

3

about them: a distorted version of the human face, with flat ape-like nose, small eyes glinting with cruelty, and a massive jaw with long yellow teeth. But the Ogrons had one quality which gave Moni a glimmer of hope, even now: for all their savage ferocity and primitive strength, they were very, very stupid.

Moni scrambled to his feet. Forcing himself to speak slowly and calmly he said, 'I am a section leader of Work Camp Three. I am needed to replace a section leader of Work Camp Four, who has been taken ill.' He looked round the circle of Ogrons to see if his story was being believed. The Ogrons looked back at him impassively. Did they believe him? Had they even understood what he was saying? In the same calm, flat voice Moni said, 'The order for my transfer came direct from your masters. If I am delayed they will be very angry. They will be angry with *you*.'

This time his words had some effect. It was almost comic to see the looks of alarm on the brutal Ogron faces. The one thing which could strike fear to the hearts of these terrifying creatures was the mention of the even more fearsome beings who were their masters.

The leading Ogron gestured into the darkness with a massive hairy paw. 'You go. Go quickly.' Moni turned and ran into the darkness.

It took him another hour of hard, dangerous travel before he reached his destination. He crossed a patch of waste ground. The moonlight showed weeds flourishing over the shattered foundations of a house. Shifting the concealing rubble, Moni found and then lifted a hidden trap-door and dropped down into the darkness. He landed at the head of a still intact flight of steps. Cautiously he moved down them until his eyes picked out a little patch of light at the bottom. It was shining beneath the edge of a closed door. Moni moved quietly to the door and rapped out a complicated series of knocks. After a moment the door creaked open. Boaz stood facing him, blaster in hand. 'All right Boaz, it's me,' said Moni.

Boaz's voice showed the strain he was feeling. 'You're late... we didn't know—'

Moni interrupted him. 'Ran straight into an Ogron patrol. Managed to talk my way out of it. The others here?' Boaz nodded, and Moni followed him into the cellar.

Anat and Shura were huddled round the charcoal fire that blazed in a makeshift brazier. Moni glanced quickly round the room. It was his first visit to the H.Q. of this particular cell, but they were all much the same. In every city there were hidden rooms like this. Places to store arms and food. Places to meet and talk and plan. Places where men and women met with one burning desire in common – to take back their planet from the alien beings who had stolen it.

Patrolling Ogrons carried out an unending search for these hideouts. Sometimes they found one: Ogron boots kicked in the door and the little group of plotters inside were ruthlessly destroyed. But for every cell that was wiped out, another and still another sprang up to replace it.

Moni looked round at the three eager faces. Boaz, dark, scowling and intense; fiercely brave, but too highly strung, too ready to act without thinking. Shura, the youngest, full of a fiery idealism. Finally, he looked at the girl, Anat. Slim, dark and wiry with close-cropped hair. Anat was still beautiful, in spite of the rough work clothes she was wearing. Here was the real leader, Moni thought. Fierce courage, a passionate hatred of the enemy, and the cunning and caution that made her wait until the best moment to strike.

Anat spoke first. 'Something's happening, Moni. What is it? You wouldn't have called this meeting without good reason. We don't often have the honour of meeting one of the Central Committee!'

Brisk and to the point as always, thought Moni approvingly. He said, 'You're right, of course, Anat. Something *has* happened. Something big, and it involves you all.' He paused for a moment, collecting his thoughts. 'You know the kind of thing we've been doing up till now – isolated bits of sabotage, sometimes big, sometimes small. But pinpricks, no more than that.'

Boaz burst out: 'Pinpricks? Is that what we've been fighting and dying for? As long as we go on hitting them, at least they know they haven't beaten us.'

Anat put a restraining hand on his arm. 'Let him talk, Boaz. He knows the value of our work.'

'You're right, of course,' said Moni quickly, 'any act of resistance is valuable in itself, but we can't go on for ever like this. They can't stop *us*, but we can't really hurt *them*. We're all losing sight of the big objective because we're too concerned with the day-to-day struggle!'

Anat said, 'Is there an alternative?'

Moni nodded. 'There may be – now. The scientists and historians of the Central Committee have come up with a plan. It's dangerous, maybe suicidal, but it offers a chance to free the entire planet. It calls for a special mission, carried out by just a handful of us. I have recommended you three for the final assault team, that is, assuming you all three volunteer.'

Anat leaned forward urgently, the glow from the fire illuminating her thin face. 'We volunteer. All of us. You know that without asking. Now, tell us the plan.'

Moni paused for a moment looking round at their eager faces. He might well be about to send them all to their deaths. He said, 'I can only give you a brief outline now. Like the rest of you, I have to be back in camp before morning. But I can tell you this much: we want to attempt to send you back through time…'

The Controller of Earth Sector One pushed aside the remains of an excellent meal. Appreciatively he drained the last of his drink – real wine in a real china cup! Few men on Earth enjoyed such luxury in *these* times. He repressed a twinge of unease at the thought of those of his fellow humans who were less fortunate, those in the work camps. They would be draining their bowls of gruel about now, desperately licking the bowls clean to see that not a scrap of food was wasted… Before leaving the room the Controller paused before a mirror, smoothing back his thinning hair and adjusting the tunic on his shoulders. More luxury, he thought. The same basic tunic as the others of course, but

7

cloth! Real cloth, none of your plastic! He picked up the sheaf of reports he had been working on through dinner and sighed. He knew how much he was envied and hated. People didn't realise that his rank had its duties too. The constant unremitting work. And now he had to make his report to Them. Something They wouldn't care to hear, what's more.

Bracing himself, the Controller left his private dining-room and strode along the endless corridors of Central Control. Scurrying human slave workers made way for him deferentially. But it was a different story when he reached the doorway leading to the innermost H.Q. The door was flanked by Ogron guards, and as he tried to enter, one of them shoved him away with a hairy paw. The Controller strove to retain his dignity.

'You know who I am. Chief Controller of this entire sector. You will show me the respect I am entitled to.' The Ogron looked at him impassively, and the Controller's shoulders drooped in defeat. He knew that the Ogron saw him as just another human. A slave, like all humans. He said dully, 'You don't understand. I must make a most important report – to your masters.' Unconsciously copying the tactics of Moni the night before, the Controller added, 'They will be angry if you do not let me enter.'

The Ogron grunted, 'You – wait!' Leaving its fellow to guard the Controller it went inside. After a moment it returned and said, 'Come now.'

The Controller went through into the antechamber and then waited. Silently a panel slid open in front of him and he entered the inner chamber.

It was a small, completely bare room with a raised ramp at one end. After a moment another wall-panel slid open and a gleaming metallic creature glided through. Its eye-stalk swung round to look at the Controller, who bowed respectfully. This, after all, was the Black Dalek, one of the supreme rulers of the planet Earth in the twenty-second century.

In its grating metallic voice the Black Dalek said, 'Report!'

The Controller tried to restrain the quaver of terror in his voice. 'I have been studying the recent reports of resistance activity. It has reached a peak in recent weeks. I think they are planning some major operation against you.'

The Black Dalek said, 'The humans you refer to as the resistance are criminals. They are enemies of the Daleks. You will find and destroy them.'

The Controller sighed. It was always the same: the flat, toneless command to do the impossible. The Daleks seemed to have no conception of the courage and cunning of the resistance, nor for that matter of the lumbering stupidity of the Ogrons they expected to catch them. He struggled on. 'There has been one particular feature of the recent wave of activity. Several recent thefts have involved papers or equipment dealing with your research into time travel.'

For a moment the Black Dalek did not reply. When it spoke its grating voice seemed to be pitched a few degrees higher. The Controller shuddered. This, he knew, was a sign of anger. The Dalek said, 'We shall maintain a continuous scan upon the Time Vortex. If the humans attempt to travel in time we shall track them down and destroy them.' The Black Dalek's voice rose higher still as it chanted the threat of destruction that was the Daleks only creed: 'They are enemies of the Daleks. All enemies of the Daleks must be destroyed. Exterminate them! EXTERMINATE THEM! EXTERMINATE THEM!'

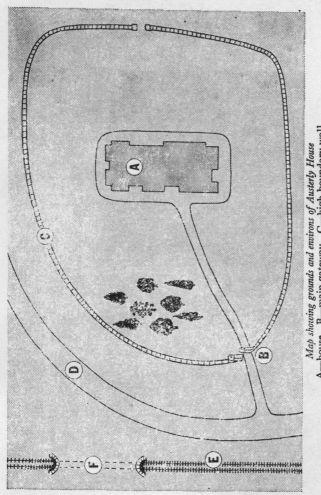

Map showing grounds and environs of Austerly House
A—house B—main gateway C—high boundary wall
D—road E—two-track railway line (disused) F—tunnel

2

The Man Who Saw a Ghost

Suddenly in the clump of trees that huddled close to the side of Austerly House an owl hooted. The UNIT sentry swung round, his Sterling sub-machine gun at the ready. Then he went on with his lonely patrol, grinning at his own nervousness. Mind you, he thought, a night like this was enough to make anyone jumpy: the wind howled eerily in the trees, black clouds streaked past the full moon, so that pitch darkness alternated with bright moonlight. And all the time he heard the mysterious night noises of the countryside. The sentry was a Londoner. He would have been far happier guarding somewhere where there was a bit of life – pavements and street lights and people passing by.

He marched along the gravel path that bordered the house. He glanced up at the rows of windows. All dark – except for one, where light showed through a gap in the curtains of the ground-floor study. Nobody could say the old boy wasn't a worker, thought the sentry. Past midnight and still at it. The sentry remembered what the Brigadier had said at the briefing meeting.

'The international situation has taken an ugly turn. There is a very real possibility that the events in the Near East will escalate into a full-scale conflict. We may well be on the verge of World War Three. The peace of the world depends on the success of the coming Conference. And the success of that Conference depends on one man – Sir Reginald Styles. His safety is in your hands.'

The peace of the world... thought the sentry. It was a big responsibility for one tall, grey-haired old man. No wonder the old boy was a bit tetchy. Still, Sir Reginald would be safe enough with sentries all round the house, more at the main gate, and patrols in the grounds. With a final glance at the study window, the sentry turned and began to retrace his steps. As he disappeared from view round the corner of the building, there was a curious shimmering in the air. Suddenly a man appeared. One moment he wasn't there, the next he was. He wore dark combat clothing – tunic, trousers, and boots. A massive hand-gun was holstered at his side. He had no badges or military insignia, but looked like a soldier... perhaps some kind of irregular, a commando or a guerilla.

The man flattened himself against the side of the building. Then he began to edge cautiously towards the lighted French windows of the study.

Inside the study all was silent except for the ticking of the clock and the scratching of Sir Reginald's pen. He was preparing the notes for his speech at the coming Conference. '*It is therefore vital,*' he wrote, '*that the Chinese Government accepts the assurances ...*'

Sir Reginald stopped writing and looked up. Had there been something at the window? A tapping, a scratching as if the latch was being slid back? No, there was nothing. It was

14

all this security nonsense making him jumpy. How could he work with soldiers clumping round the house. He began writing again. '… *accepts the assurances of good faith* …'

The sound came again. Sir Reginald stood up… maybe one of the sentries was trying the window. Sir Reginald called, 'Who is it? Who's there?' No answer. He strode to the French windows and threw them open.

Facing him was a youngish man in some kind of guerilla uniform. The man was holding an enormous pistol, trained straight at Sir Reginald's head. It was many years since Sir Reginald had been a soldier but the old reflexes still worked. He flung himself upon the man, dragging down the gun arm. He hung on desperately as the guerilla thrust him back into the room. The two men reeled about, sending the lamp crashing from the desk. They tripped and fell over a chair, smashing it beneath them. Sir Reginald hung on to his attacker's gun arm with both hands, desperately trying to get control of the weapon. There could be only one end to the unequal struggle: Sir Reginald was well into his sixties, the guerilla young and strong. Pinning the old man beneath him he slowly brought his gun round to aim at his victim's head. Despite all his efforts, Sir Reginald saw the muzzle of the gun pointing straight at him… he could see and feel everything with a strange clarity, as if it were happening in slow motion… the circle of the gun barrel looked enormous… above it he could see the guerilla's face twisted with savage hatred. He could even see the man's knuckles begin to whiten as his finger tightened on the trigger. He wrenched at the guerilla's sinewy wrist with both hands, but it was as firm as

15

a rock. His hands were slipping. Then, incredibly, they were empty. The guerilla's wrist seemed to melt away. The whole figure of his opponent shimmered, then vanished. As the study door was flung open Sir Reginald found himself flat on his back wrestling with thin air. A UNIT corporal helped Sir Reginald to his feet; he was trembling with reaction and shock. Miss Paget, his secretary, went to him.

She said, 'Sir Reginald, what happened? Are you all right?'

Sir Reginald looked at her wildly. 'Attacked me… he attacked me. Tried to kill me!'

One of the patrolling sentries stood outside the French windows. The corporal rapped. 'See anyone?'

The sentry shook his head. 'Came running when I heard the noise, Corp. No one came through there.'

The corporal turned back to Sir Reginald. '*Who* attacked you, sir? Who did you see?'

Sir Reginald said slowly: 'He vanished… disappeared into thin air… like a ghost…'

Brigadier Alastair Lethbridge-Stewart swung his highly-polished boots onto the top of his desk, tucked the telephone receiver under his chin and waited for the Minister to stop yammering in his ear.

The Brigadier glanced at the headlines on the front page of *The Times* – 'NEAR EAST CRISIS – WAR LOOMS'. If it happened he'd apply to be posted back to his Regiment. It would be nice to wear the kilt again. The Brigadier realised that the voice in his ear had stopped. He said, 'Er, quite, sir. Quite.' The yammering started up again. The Brigadier sighed, interrupting politely, but firmly.

'I have the reports in front of me now, sir. The sentry *outside* the house heard the sounds of struggle, and ran towards the French windows. The sentry *inside* the house also heard the noise and ran through the study door. Except for Sir Reginald himself, the study was empty.' There was a further outburst on the other end of the 'phone. The Brigadier replied, 'No, sir, I was not proposing to ignore the matter!' Since he had in fact been proposing to do exactly that, he had to pause and rack his brains for a moment before going on. Then inspiration came.

'As a matter of fact, sir,' said the Brigadier, lying magnificently, 'I was about to pass the matter over to one of my top men.' The Brigadier allowed a hint of reproach to creep into his voice – 'I was just on my way to brief him when you called...'

Inside the laboratory of the Scientific Adviser to UNIT everything was still. Mysterious tangles of elaborate equipment straggled over the benches. The solid blue shape of an old police box stood incongruously in one corner. Suddenly the police box began to give out the most agonising groaning sound. It vibrated, shaking the whole laboratory and rattling the retorts and test tubes. The groaning reached a peak, there was a loud bang, the door of the police box burst open, and a tall, lean man shot out of the police box in a cloud of smoke. He slammed the door behind him, cursing fluently in an obscure Martian dialect.

The laboratory door opened. A very small, very pretty girl came in. Quite unsurprised she slapped the coughing Doctor on the back, gave him a glass of water and opened the laboratory window to let out the smoke.

'Foiled again, Doctor?' asked Jo Grant sympathetically.

The Doctor nodded, sipping his water gloomily. 'It's maddening. I'm so nearly there. If I could only cut out their primary override on the dematerialisation circuit.' He picked up a sheaf of notes and studied them gloomily.

Jo looked at him affectionately. Sometimes the Doctor seemed to think she understood the most difficult scientific theories as easily as he did himself. At other times he had an infuriating habit of carefully explaining that two and two made four.

When she had first joined UNIT, Jo Grant had assumed that the Doctor's story of travelling in Time and Space in a police box called the TARDIS (the initials stood for 'Time and Relative Dimensions in Space') was some kind of joke. Recent experiences had changed all that. The TARDIS, temporarily 'grounded' by decree of the Doctor's mysterious superiors, the Time Lords, had suddenly started working again and Jo had found herself caught up in an adventure on another planet in the distant future.* With this in mind she said:

'I thought the TARDIS was working again!'

'My dear Jo, the TARDIS was being operated under remote-control by the Time Lords… just because they wanted me to do their dirty work for them!'

* *Doctor Who and the Doomsday Weapon*

18

'But if it works for *them*—' Jo persisted.

'I don't want it to work for *them*,' said the Doctor irritably, 'I want it to work for *me*. No one's going to use me as an interplanetary puppet.'

Suddenly, an inspiration seemed to strike him. 'Of course. Now why didn't I think of that earlier.'

Leaping up, the Doctor dashed back inside the TARDIS. Through its open doors Jo could see that he was bent over the central control column, making careful adjustments to the instruments. As he did so the laboratory door opened. Jo looked up and to her utter astonishment saw the Doctor standing in the doorway.

Amazed, she looked back inside the TARDIS. There was the Doctor still bending over the console. She looked back at the door. There was the Doctor standing looking at her. But there was an even bigger shock to come. Another figure appeared from behind the Doctor. She was looking at herself.

The two Jo Grants looked at each other in mutual astonishment. Then the Doctor, the one in the doorway, spoke.

'Good grief! Oh yes… yes, of course. I remember now.'

He gave Jo his familiar charming smile. But she could only gaze back at him thunderstruck, as he said reassuringly, 'Now don't worry, my dear. I know you're alarmed, but…'

He was interrupted by the appearance of the Doctor from inside the TARDIS. But this Doctor shared none of Jo's astonishment. He looked at his other self with a sort of mild curiosity… 'Oh no! What are *you* doing here?'

The new arrival rubbed his chin and said apologetically, 'Don't worry, I'm not here… that is… well in a sense I am here, but you're not there. It's all a bit complicated to explain…'

The Doctor cut his other self short. 'Well this won't do at all, will it? Can't have two of us running about.'

'Don't worry, old chap,' said the second Doctor cheerily. 'It'll all be—'

And then he vanished in mid-sentence, the second Jo Grant with him. The remaining Doctor gave a satisfied nod, and headed back inside the TARDIS.

'Now just a minute, Doctor,' Jo protested. 'What was all *that* about?'

'I'm afraid I must have overloaded the temporal circuitry, Jo. Must have produced a localised distortion.'

Jo looked at him, still baffled. The Doctor chuckled. 'Very funny thing, Time. Once you start tampering with it, the oddest things happen.'

Jo said: 'But there was another me – and another you. Where did they go?'

'Back into their own time stream of course. Or do I mean forward?'

Jo made a final protest. 'But Doctor…'

The Doctor waved her aside reassuringly. 'Don't worry, my dear. Just a freak effect. Now I really must get on.'

He was just about to re-enter the TARDIS when the door opened once more. Jo looked up in alarm, but this time it was only the Brigadier. 'So there you are, Doctor. I need your help.' Jo could see that the Doctor was not very pleased by this new interruption. She braced herself for the inevitable clash.

'I'm sorry, Brigadier,' said the Doctor curtly. 'I happen to be extremely busy.'

'So am I, Doctor. Now then, you've heard of Sir Reginald Styles?'

'No,' said the Doctor flatly. He picked up his notes and began to study them.

Jo said helpfully, 'Isn't he the chief British representative at the United Nations?'

'That's right, Miss Grant. And he's the key man in the latest summit conference.'

The Doctor looked up. 'My dear Brigadier, I'm a scientist, not a politician.'

With an exasperated sigh the Brigadier retorted, 'If you weren't always tinkering with that wretched contraption of yours, perhaps you'd realise just how bad the international situation has become.'

'You humans are always squabbling over something,' remarked the Doctor pointedly.

'This particular squabble looks very like ending up in a third world war.'

There was real anxiety in the Brigadier's voice. The Doctor's attitude changed at once. 'As bad as that, old chap?'

The Brigadier sank down onto a laboratory stool. 'The whole thing flared up in the Near East. But really it's a sort of three-cornered quarrel between Russia, America, and China. Sphere of influence, that sort of thing.'

'And Britain arranged for this summit conference,' said Jo, 'so that the three big powers could meet and sort it all out.'

'Exactly, Miss Grant. But at the last moment the Chinese refused to attend. Without them the conference can't even start. Sir Reginald Styles is due to fly to Peking in a few hours' time.

The Chinese trust him. There's just a chance he may be able to persuade them to change their minds.'

Tossing aside his sheaf of notes the Doctor said, 'All right, Brigadier. You've convinced me the situation's serious. Where do *I* come in?'

'Styles has suddenly started acting oddly. Last night he claimed someone tried to kill him at his home. This morning he denies the whole thing. You see the problem, Doctor. If Styles doesn't fly to Peking, the conference may fail. But how can we let him go if he's cracking up?'

'Suppose he isn't cracking up?' said Jo. 'Suppose his story's true?'

'That's just it. According to my men, no one was there. No one could have been there.'

Briefly, the Brigadier recounted the events of the previous night.

The Doctor looked thoughtful. 'From what you say of Styles, he's not the type to invent or imagine things. So obviously *something* happened. The question is what? Did Styles say anything more – last night, I mean?'

The Brigadier shrugged. 'Apparently he just babbled something about a ghost.'

In a clearing in the woods near Austerly House there was a sudden shimmering and distortion in the air. Then a man appeared! One moment he wasn't there, the next he was. He wore the tough, serviceable clothes of a guerilla, and there was a massive hand-gun holstered at his side.

The man looked swiftly around him. He heard movement

nearby, and with a swift, practised movement flung himself to the ground, rolling into the cover of a patch of bracken. Seconds later the boots of a UNIT patrol passed within inches of his head. When the patrol had gone on its way, the man got to his feet. He began to move cautiously through the trees towards the house. Then, directly ahead of him, came another shimmering in the air. Three huge forms materialised, blocking his path. The guerilla's mind was filled with panic. Ogrons! They had pursued him from his own time.

Abandoning any attempt at silence, the guerilla turned and ran away from the direction of the house. He heard the sound of the pursuing Ogrons as they crashed through the woods behind him. He knew he could outrun them, at least for a while. Their huge bulk made them slow and clumsy. But he knew, too, that the Ogrons' endurance was almost limitless. When he was utterly worn out and breathless they would still be lumbering after him. And if they caught him... instant death – if he was lucky; otherwise capture, and a return to his own time zone for interrogation by the Daleks. His only chance was to lose the Ogrons in a sudden burst of speed.

The guerilla burst from the edge of the woods into open park land. The going was easier here. Easier too, for his pursuers. They were still behind him. Just ahead a high wall marked the edge of the grounds. With a desperate spurt of speed he ran towards it. The three Ogrons appeared behind him in close pursuit.

Meanwhile a third group had joined the chase. Sergeant

23

Benton of UNIT had been outraged to have the peace of a routine patrol disturbed by what sounded like a herd of elephants crashing through the woods. He led his patrol at a fast trot towards the sound. As they ran they unslung their Sterling sub-machine guns.

The fleeing guerilla reached the wall and hurled himself at the top in a desperate, scrabbling leap. For a moment he hung by his hands from the top of the wall, then, slowly and painfully, managed to heave himself over.

Benton and his patrol emerged from the woods just in time to see the guerilla drop down out of sight. They watched in amazement as the pursuing Ogrons swarmed over the wall with ape-like ease and also disappeared from view. Benton yelled: 'After them!' adding to himself, 'Whatever they are.' The UNIT patrol sprinted for the wall and began to scale it.

The guerilla was panting and gasping now, beginning to slow down. Getting over the wall had cost him time, and the Ogrons were very close. Across the field in front of him he could see a fenced-off strip of land running parallel to the road. Two steel rails ran along the centre of it. Of course – a railway! Some primitive twentieth century transport system. Not far away the rails disappeared into a dark archway. A tunnel. He could hide in its darkness, use the time transmitter and get back to his own time… He was almost within reach of the tunnel mouth when his foot twisted on a stone. He crashed to the ground, half-stunned.

With a savage roar of triumph, the pursuing Ogrons were upon him. He struggled to rise but his leg gave way beneath him. The huge hairy hands of the Ogrons reached out for him, and a massive blow smashed him to the ground.

Benton and his patrol came running up. 'Give 'em a warning shot!' snapped Benton. A burst of machine-gun fire rattled over the Ogrons' heads. One of the Ogrons drew the strange, massive pistol from the holster at its side and fired back. There was a sharp electronic buzz, and the man next to Sergeant Benton simply disintegrated. He vanished, as though his whole being had exploded into fragments.

'Take cover!' yelled Benton, and the UNIT soldiers hurled themselves to the ground, rolling into whatever shelter they could find. A burst of fire hammered into the Ogrons. The creatures staggered under the impact of the bullets, but did not fall. At a sign from their leader they fled into the darkness of the tunnel mouth, leaving the crumpled form of their prisoner behind them.

The UNIT patrol dashed up to the tunnel. 'One of you look after him,' ordered Benton, indicating the unconscious guerilla. 'You two, cover the other end of that tunnel. Whatever those things are, we've got them bottled up.' Cautiously, with guns at the ready, Benton and his men advanced into the blackness of the tunnel.

3

The Vanishing Guerilla

In Sir Reginald's study at Austerly House, the Doctor, the Brigadier, and Jo Grant were hearing an account of the events of the previous night. Miss Paget, Sir Reginald's secretary, was a thin, sharp-featured woman in her fifties, the perfect picture of the top-ranking senior secretary. It was obvious that she was devoted to Sir Reginald, and had been very shaken by his strange behaviour.

'Please go on, Miss Paget,' said the Doctor in his most reassuring voice.

'I think that's everything really. Sir Reginald *said* someone attacked him. But there just wasn't anyone there.'

'And he definitely used the word "ghost"?'

'Oh yes. I was quite struck by it. You see, he's always been very scornful of—'

Miss Paget stopped talking as though she'd been switched off. Sir Reginald stalked into the room. He looked round angrily.

'What's going on here?'

'These gentlemen are from UNIT,' said Miss Paget.

'And who asked them to come here? We've got enough soldiers cluttering up the place as it is.'

Miss Paget's voice was shaky but determined. 'I asked them, Sir Reginald. Because of what happened last night.'

'Nothing happened last night,' said Styles icily.

Crushed, Miss Paget was silent.

The Brigadier said firmly: 'There does appear to have been *some* sort of incident, Sir Reginald.'

Sir Reginald was obviously not used to being contradicted. He looked as if he might explode at any moment.

Tactfully, Jo Grant said, 'Perhaps if *you* could tell us what really happened, Sir Reginald?' She gave him her most charming smile.

Sir Reginald was too well-mannered to storm at what appeared to be a mere child. Wearily he said, 'I was working late – must have nodded off at my desk. I knocked over the lamp, scattered all my papers. I woke up a little confused. I was picking up my papers when Miss Paget and the sentry came in. All a lot of fuss about nothing.'

Sir Reginald wasn't used to lying, and he did it very badly. Jo couldn't help feeling sorry for him as he gazed fiercely round, trying to hang on to his dignity.

The Doctor meanwhile had wandered over to the French windows, and seemed to be studying the pattern of the carpet. The Brigadier persisted, 'But you did mention ghosts, Sir Reginald.'

'Did I? Must have been having a bit of a nightmare.'

The Doctor said gently, 'What about these marks here?' He pointed downward. 'Muddy feet, Sir Reginald. Someone *was* here.'

'Must have been the sentry.'

28

The Doctor shook his head. 'According to Miss Paget the outside sentry didn't come into the room.'

Sir Reginald blustered, 'Are you accusing me of lying, sir?'

Hastily the Brigadier cut in, 'You've obviously been under a good deal of strain, sir. Were you feeling at all unwell last night?'

Sir Reginald snapped: 'Felt, and feel, perfectly well. Now, if you'll excuse me, Brigadier, I really can't afford to waste any more time.' He turned to Miss Paget. 'Where's that car? I'm due at the airport in twenty minutes.'

Miss Paget said, 'It's waiting for you now, sir.'

Jo saw the Brigadier look quickly at the Doctor. She sensed the unspoken question. The Doctor said, 'Then we mustn't detain you further, Sir Reginald. Allow me to wish you every success in your mission.'

For a moment Sir Reginald seemed taken aback. Then, with a brief nod of farewell he turned and left the room, Miss Paget scuttling behind him. Captain Yates, the Brigadier's number two, appeared in the doorway. 'Call for you on the RT, sir. Sergeant Benton.'

As the Brigadier went out into the hall, Jo turned to the Doctor. 'What was all that about? Something did happen last night, didn't it?'

The Doctor nodded.

'Then why did Sir Reginald say that it didn't?'

'My dear Jo,' said the Doctor gently, 'whatever happened was so extraordinary that Sir Reginald can't believe it. He thinks he's been having hallucinations.'

'So why doesn't he admit it?'

The Doctor sighed. 'If you were about to begin an important mission would you want to admit you'd been seeing things?'

'I see,' said Jo brightly. 'So that's why you pretended to believe him.'

'Nothing else to be done. He's been shaken up, but he's still perfectly capable. And at the moment this little planet of yours needs his talents very badly.'

The Brigadier appeared in the doorway. 'Doctor, Miss Grant, will you come with me, please? There's been some kind of shooting incident just outside the grounds.'

As Jo, the Doctor and the Brigadier came down the steps at the front of Austerly House they saw Sir Reginald's limousine drawing away. The Brigadier looked after the car for a moment, strain and anxiety plain on his face. Then he bustled Jo and the Doctor into the waiting jeep. Captain Yates started the engine and they shot off, gravel spurting from beneath their wheels.

Five minutes' fast driving brought them to the road near the railway tunnel.

An anxious-looking Sergeant Benton was waiting for them.

'Morning, Sergeant Benton,' said Jo cheerily. But Benton was too worried to give her more than a quick nod.

'This way, sir,' he said, and led them across the fields to the tunnel.

On the way he told his story to the extremely sceptical Brigadier. Jo couldn't help feeling sorry for him as he struggled on. The Brigadier interrupted, 'Let me see if I've got it straight, Benton. This chap appeared from nowhere, and these other – creatures were chasing him?'

Benton said, 'That's right, sir. Sort of ape-like they were. Like stone-age men, or gorillas.'

'I see. Gorillas wearing clothes and carrying guns?' drawled the Brigadier.

Benton nodded dumbly.

'Then where the blazes are they, Sergeant Benton? You said you had them trapped in the tunnel. Presumably you captured or killed them all?'

Benton swallowed hard. 'Well no, sir. We had men going in from both ends. The two patrols bumped into each other. The tunnel was empty.'

'You saw them go in, you sealed off both ends, and the tunnel was empty?' said the Brigadier incredulously.

Again Benton nodded. 'Some kind of trap-door,' said the Brigadier hopefully. 'Maybe a secret passage?'

Benton shook his head. 'We checked, sir. Every inch. It's just a plain, ordinary railway tunnel. Not even used any more. This line was shut down years ago.'

The Doctor was bending over the unconscious man in guerilla's clothes. 'This chap's in a pretty bad way. Concussion, I think. He should be in hospital.'

'Ambulance is already on its way, Doctor,' said Benton. 'We'll get him to the UNIT sick-bay.'

The Brigadier picked up the strange-looking gun lying by the guerilla's side. 'What do you make of this, Doctor?'

The Doctor examined it curiously. 'It's a new one on me,

Brigadier. But at the moment I'm rather more interested in this. It was hidden inside his tunic.'

The Doctor held out a small black box with control knobs set into the top. Jo thought it looked like a rather superior transistor radio.

'Some kind of signalling device?' suggested the Brigadier.

The Doctor shook his head. 'As a matter of fact, Brigadier, I think it's a rather primitive form of time machine.'

There was the rhythmic blare of a siren, and they saw a UNIT ambulance driving along the road. It stopped. Two men jumped out carrying a stretcher. The Brigadier turned to Sergeant Benton. 'See him into the ambulance, Sergeant. You'd better travel with him. Take a couple of men with you. I want him kept under constant guard.'

Benton saluted, waved over the ambulance men, then started to transfer the wounded guerilla to the vehicle. The man was muttering and groaning as they lifted him onto the stretcher.

'Do you think he'll be all right, Doctor?' asked Jo.

The Doctor was still absorbed in the strange black box. 'Oh I think so, Jo.'

'As soon as he recovers consciousness,' said the Brigadier grimly, 'he'll have quite a few explanations to make.'

The Doctor looked up. 'No doubt. Meanwhile, we've found two very interesting clues. That gun of his, and this machine. Let's get back to the laboratory, Jo. I think I'd like to run one or two tests…'

*

The office of the Controller of Earth Sector One was not a pleasant or comfortable place, just bare gleaming metal walls and floor, and a plain functional desk. But to the Controller himself it was evidence of his power and rank. Few humans enjoyed such space and luxury. But after all, he reminded himself, he was the supreme authority in that part of Earth once known as England. Supreme after the Daleks, of course...

Coldly, the Controller studied the Ogron guard. There was a cutting edge in his voice when he spoke. 'You have failed in your mission.'

The Ogron shook its head vigorously. There was almost a tremor in the thick guttural voice as it replied. Ogrons could master human speech only with difficulty, and their vocabularies were very small.

The Ogron growled, 'No, Controller, we did not fail. We found the enemy and destroyed him.'

'You were told to capture him alive. He was needed for interrogation.'

'Human soldiers came. We had to return to this time zone.'

Wearily, the Controller wondered if the Ogron was telling the truth. The creatures were so savage that it was difficult to persuade them to take prisoners. Their instinct was to kill anyone they got their hands on.

'Then you are sure the rebel was dead? If the twentieth century humans captured him alive, he could tell them much.'

There was a flicker of fear in the Ogron's tiny red eyes. It grunted, 'The enemy is dead. We killed him.'

The Controller rose from behind his desk. 'I want an intensified effort by all your patrols. These rebellious criminals must be found and destroyed! If not – the Daleks will be displeased. They will punish you. Now go!'

The Ogron lumbered from the room. The Controller sighed. For years now the criminal rebels – guerillas they called themselves – had been resisting the rule of the Daleks. Never more than a pitiful handful of them. Yet in a way, that handful seemed immortal. As soon as one group of resistance fighters was tracked down another sprang up. With their pitifully tiny resources, their cellar hideouts and their home-made weapons they took on all the might of the Dalek technology. Naturally, the rebels could never win. Yet in a way it seemed they could never lose. The Controller was forced almost to admire his fellow humans. They were wrong, of course. Hopelessly misguided. But such courage! Such persistence and cunning in the face of impossible odds. With qualities like these it was easy to see why the race of Man had once been a great one. The Controller sighed again. But it was ultimately all for nothing. Eventually the rebels would lose the unequal fight. They would suffer the fate of everyone who opposed the Daleks. They would be exterminated.

With a deliberate effort the Controller turned his attention back to his duties. The production figures for Work Camp Three were below the norm. If they did not improve the Daleks would be angry. The Controller began to study the sheaf of production reports on his desk.

*

As the Brigadier strode into the UNIT laboratory he was astonished to see Jo Grant hauling a large stuffed dummy across the laboratory. She propped it up in a chair at the far end of the room, and stood back, looking at her work in satisfaction.

'Bit early for Guy Fawkes' Night, Miss Grant,' said the Brigadier.

Jo turned at the sound of his voice. 'The Doctor wanted it. Don't ask me why. How's that poor man you found?'

The Brigadier shrugged. 'Benton's with him in sickbay now. Chap's still out cold, apparently. Will be for some time.'

The Doctor emerged from the TARDIS, the guerilla's gun in one hand, the black box in the other. 'Then we'll just have to wait till he wakes up, won't we?' His tone was brisk and cheerful... Jo saw that he was thoroughly enjoying the task of grappling with this new problem. She couldn't help feeling glad that he'd found something to take his mind from the endless and seemingly hopeless struggle to get the TARDIS working again. The Doctor looked at Jo's dummy slumped grotesquely on its chair at the far end of the laboratory.

'Splendid, Jo. Just what I wanted. Most lifelike, isn't it, Brigadier?'

The Brigadier studied the drooping dummy without enthusiasm. 'Yes, very nice. May I ask what it's in aid of?'

'I thought you might like a little practical demonstration. Now then, if you'll all step this way.'

The Doctor led them to a position by the door. At

the opposite end of the laboratory, the dummy slumped grotesquely in its chair. The body was made from an old pair of army denims stuffed with newspapers. It had a paper-stuffed pillowslip for a head. Jo had drawn a crude grinning face on the pillowslip with lipstick.

'Now, Jo, Brigadier,' said the Doctor, 'I think you'd better stand behind me – just in case.' He raised the guerilla's gun, and aimed it at the dummy.

'Steady on, Doctor,' said the Brigadier hurriedly. 'Just in case of *what*, exactly?'

The Doctor looked over his shoulder. 'In case I've mistimed the setting, of course. In which case, we might lose most of the wall.'

The Brigadier was outraged. 'Now just a moment! This building happens to be Government prop—'

But he was already too late. The Doctor had resumed his aim, and activated some kind of trigger. There was a high-pitched electronic buzz. Chair and dummy simply vanished! The Doctor gave a satisfied nod.

The Brigadier walked slowly to the other end of the laboratory. There was absolutely no sign of either chair or dummy. He looked at the gun in the Doctor's hand. 'What the blazes is that thing, Doctor?'

The Doctor put the gun down on a laboratory bench. 'Quite an effective little weapon, isn't it?'

The Brigadier looked grim. 'According to Benton those ape creatures were carrying exactly the same kind of weapon. He lost one of his men. No trace of the body afterwards.'

The Brigadier's voice was angry. Jo knew how much he

worried about the safety of the men under his command. To lose even one soldier was a considerable blow.

Gingerly, Jo picked up the alien weapon. It looked something like a cross between a revolver and a blunderbuss. It was heavy, and she needed two hands to hold it.

'What is it exactly, Doctor?' she asked. 'I mean, how does it work?'

'Basically, it's a form of ultrasonic disintegrator.'

Jo tried to translate the Doctor's reply into something she could understand. 'You mean it's some kind of ray-gun?'

The Doctor took a deep breath. 'Er, well, yes, Jo. Sort of... The point is, it's an extremely sophisticated weapon. Far more advanced than anything yet developed on Earth. Er – I don't think you'd better point it like that.'

Jo realised that she was aiming the gun straight at the Brigadier. Hastily she put it back on the bench.

The Brigadier said, 'You say it wasn't made on Earth? You mean it comes from another planet?'

The Doctor shook his head. 'I've just done a metallurgical analysis: it proved conclusively that the metal from which this gun was made was mined here on Earth.'

Jo was puzzled. 'But you said it couldn't have been made on Earth.'

'Not at the present time, Jo.'

'Kindly stop talking in riddles, Doctor,' said the Brigadier irritably.

The Doctor walked to the other end of the bench and picked up the black box. 'Do you believe in ghosts, Brigadier?'

'Do let's be serious.'

'I am serious, I assure you. Perhaps I used the wrong word: not so much ghosts as apparitions – creatures that can appear and disappear.' He studied the box, turning it round in his hands. 'You see we usually think of ghosts as coming from the past. But what about ghosts from the future?'

He looked from Jo to the Brigadier, smiling gently at the sight of their baffled faces.

Jo said slowly, 'You said that thing was some kind of time machine…'

The Doctor picked up the little machine and began fiddling with the controls. 'That's right. But I think it must have been damaged when the man fell. I can't seem to get it to…'

But even as the Doctor spoke the machine seemed to come to life. It gave a sort of low hum. A curious shimmering effect filled the air around it.

The Doctor shouted, 'Good grief, it's working! Stand back both of you!' Frantically he jabbed at the control knobs.

In the UNIT sick-bay, not far away, Sergeant Benton sat beside the unconscious guerilla's bed. The guerilla, now wearing a pair of hospital pyjamas, was twisting and muttering, drifting in and out of a kind of coma. Not long ago he had suddenly shouted in fear, then slumped back into unconsciousness. For the moment he was relatively quiet. Benton's head began to nod, as he was lulled by the peace of the little room. Suddenly Benton jerked awake. A strange shimmering seemed to fill the air. Benton looked on in utter amazement as the guerilla simply faded away. The shimmering stopped and the bed was empty. Benton found himself pulling back the sheets and peering under the pillow, as if he expected to find the man hiding. Then he pulled himself together. The bloke was gone, and that was that. Benton sighed. Guess who'd have to try and explain *that* to the Brigadier...

The Controller of Earth Sector One stood in the Temporal Scanning Room. All around him was the strange and mysterious machinery of the Daleks keeping continuous watch on the Time Vortex, that mysterious void where Time and Space are one. Girl technicians moved silently about the room. The Controller thought to himself that there was something strange and inhuman about them. They seemed completely emotionless, dedicated to the machines they served. He turned to the girl beside him and said, 'Why did you send for me?'

The girl indicated a faint flickering pulse on one of the screens in front of them. 'A time transmitter is in operation in the twentieth century time zone.'

The Controller felt a sudden excitement. This could only mean more resistance activity. This time, perhaps, he could trap them. He said, 'Can you fix the Space Time co-ordinates?'

Coldly the girl said, 'I will try. The trace is very faint.'

Her hands flickered quickly over the controls on the console in front of her. Slowly the pulse on the screen flickered and died.

The girl said, 'It's no use, Controller. Transmission has stopped. I think a transference has taken place, but it is not possible to be specific.' Her voice was flat and unemotional. She was simply reporting a fact.

The girl's indifference only increased the Controller's feeling of anger and disappointment. Sharply he said, 'Continue scanning. Next time I advise you to be more efficient, or it will be the worse for you.'

The girl was completely unimpressed. In the same emotionless voice she said, 'Everything possible was done. We shall continue scanning. If further transmissions take place you will be informed.' She turned away and returned to her duties.

The Controller looked after her furiously. Then he sighed, accepting defeat, and left the scanning room.

In the UNIT laboratory the Doctor put the machine down with a sigh of relief. 'It's all right. The thing's gone completely dead again.'

'But it *was* working,' said Jo anxiously.

The Doctor sighed. 'Oh yes. Unfortunately it was accidental. I still don't know how or why.'

The telephone rang and the Brigadier snatched it up. 'Yes? All right, Benton, what is it?' The Brigadier's voice rose to a sort of strangled yelp. 'What! He did *what*, Benton?'

The Brigadier listened a moment longer and said, 'All right, Sergeant, I believe you. Yes, I'll tell him.' With a mighty effort he put the 'phone down, slowly and gently. 'That was

Benton from the sick-bay. You may be interested to know, Doctor, that at exactly the moment you started tinkering with that wretched machine, our guerilla friend shimmered, and vanished – just faded away out of his hospital bed.'

'Now that *is* interesting,' said the Doctor. 'What's more it proves I was right. The thing's definitely a time transmitter. Somehow I managed to shoot the poor chap back to where he came from.'

The Brigadier gave him an exasperated look. 'I'm glad you find it interesting, Doctor – but it's not particularly helpful is it? When that man vanished, our chance of finding out what's going on vanished with him.'

'Don't be so pessimistic, old chap. This business isn't over yet, you know.'

'It isn't?' said the Brigadier gloomily.

'I very much doubt it. You see, I don't think those behind it have achieved their objectives yet. So they're bound to try again.'

'Try *what* again?'

'I'm not sure about the *what*, Brigadier, but I think I know the *where!*'

The Brigadier said, 'Well, I suppose that's something.'

'Everything that's happened,' the Doctor went on, 'seems to centre round Austerly House. And who ever tried to harm Styles is certain to try again.'

'But he isn't even there! He's in Peking by now.'

'That's right. So the place will be empty.' The Doctor turned to Jo who had been looking on in puzzlement. 'Well, Jo, how about it?'

'How about what?'

The Doctor smiled. 'How do you fancy spending a night in a haunted house?'

4

The Ghost Hunters

Once again the wind whistled eerily in the trees round Austerly House. Once again a nervous sentry jumped at the sudden hoot of an owl. And, once again, one solitary window was illuminated, that of Sir Reginald Styles' ground-floor study.

Inside the study, however, things were very different. Instead of Sir Reginald toiling over his papers, the elegant figure of the Doctor lay sprawled at his ease in an armchair by the blazing log fire. On a little table beside him stood a heavy silver tray. It held knives, plates, glasses, a little basket of biscuits, a bottle of wine and a very large Stilton cheese. The little black box, the time machine, stood on the table next to the tray.

Jo Grant stood beside the Doctor's chair. The Doctor looked up at her.

'You know, Jo,' he said thoughtfully, helping himself to a large slice of cheese, 'you can always be sure of one thing with politicians whatever their political ideas: they always keep a well-stocked larder.'

Jo looked at the loaded tray with an air of some disapproval. 'I'm not sure that you really ought to help

yourself like that,' she said dubiously.

'Nonsense, Jo. You heard what Miss Paget said. We're to consider the place our own.' The Doctor took another bite of cheese by way of underlining the point.

Jo looked around uneasily. In spite of the warmth and comfort of the firelit study she was very much aware that the rest of the big, old house was dark and empty. And outside the house itself was the black night, with strange noises coming from the gloomy woods. Of course, Captain Yates, Sergeant Benton and armed UNIT patrols were guarding the house. But that hadn't helped Styles. He'd still been attacked.

Jo shivered. 'I wish you hadn't sent all the servants away.'

The Doctor poured himself a glass of Burgundy. He held

up the glass to admire the rich red colour of the wine. 'Had to be done, Jo. How can you expect ghosts to walk in a house full of people?'

Jo shivered again and the Doctor stopped his teasing. 'Look, there's really nothing to worry about. Have a piece of this delicious cheese.'

'No thanks, Doctor. I don't seem to be hungry right now.' Jo came and perched herself on the arm of his chair.

Munching away at his cheese the Doctor said indistinctly, 'Really ought to eat something, it's liable to be a long night.'

Jo said, 'I know. That's what I'm worrying about.'

Outside the house the wind howled and it was starting to rain. Captain Yates stood in the shelter of the main doorway and watched the wind thrashing about in the tree tops. Sergeant Benton hurried around the corner of the building and joined him. Benton's army waterproof was spotted with big drops of rain.

'Everything quiet, Benton?'

'Yes, sir, quiet as the grave.' Benton shuddered, wishing he'd found a more cheerful expression.

'Right, carry on.'

Benton saluted and plunged back into the darkness.

Throughout the grounds little patrols of armed men moved quietly through the pitch-black night, exchanging pre-arranged signals and passwords.

There were no sentries around the abandoned railway tunnel. It was some way from the house, and it hadn't struck the Brigadier that there was any point in guarding it.

Inside the darkness of the tunnel there came a faint shimmering and glowing. Three figures materialised one by one. First the girl, Anat, leader of the resistance cell that Moni had visited at such peril. Next Boaz, scowling with grim determination. Finally Shura, young and eager, trembling with nervous excitement. All three were loaded down with equipment.

Once all three were materialised, Anat produced a tiny light-cell. Dimly it illuminated the rough brickwork of the tunnel. Boaz said exultantly, 'We made it, Anat. We made it!'

Swiftly they began to unload the heavier equipment. Shura found a hiding place for it, a crevice in the wall of the tunnel. He covered the equipment with loose rubble, and looked up excitedly. 'Well, this is it!'

Anat was more cautious. 'The place *looks* right. But the tiniest error in the temporal co-ordinates and we may be too soon. Or too late.'

Shura said, 'There's no chance of that. We'll succeed this time.'

'We've got to,' said Anat grimly. 'Now listen to me, all of you. You heard what Moni said before we left. We're the last chance. Two others have tried before us and failed. The Daleks are getting closer all the time, and they can track our equipment. If we fail, we'll be lucky to get back to our own time zone alive. And we'll have lost the chance of defeating the Daleks.'

Boaz said, 'We won't fail, Anat.'

46

'We mustn't,' Shura added eagerly.

Anat said, 'We'll make our way to the house. You've all memorised the old historical maps?' The others nodded. She went on, 'Remember it'll be very different outside the tunnel. You'll see fields, roads, houses with people in them. The kind of world we should have had. The kind of world we can still have if we succeed. Are you both ready?'

Again the two men nodded. 'Then we'll make our way to the house. There'll be army patrols, but we'll avoid them.'

Boaz said fiercely, 'If they try to stop us…' He patted the holstered gun at his side.

Anat cut in, 'Remember, they are not our enemies. We have only one enemy. The man we have come to kill.'

Swiftly and silently the three guerillas slipped out of the tunnel and began moving across the fields to Austerly House.

The Doctor took another appreciative sip of his Burgundy. 'Ah, yes. A most good-humoured wine, this. A touch of the sardonic perhaps, but not cynical. A truly civilised little wine, one after my own heart.'

Jo looked at him impatiently. 'Do stop chuntering on, Doctor.' She got out of her chair and moved to the door. 'I'm going to the kitchen to make myself a cup of tea.'

The hallway was empty and dark. There were suits of armour by the staircase and a stuffed stag's head stared glassily at her from the wall. Everything looked strange and sinister in the gloom.

Jo was making for the kitchen when suddenly the massive

47

front door began to creak. She tried to call to the Doctor, but her voice seemed to have gone. Terrified she crouched against the wall as the door swung open. A huge figure loomed in the doorway. With a sigh of relief Jo realised it was Sergeant Benton.

In the darkness outside, the three guerillas had come to the high wall surrounding Austerly House. Working with trained efficiency they climbed it and dropped to the other side. All three froze into cover, face downward. Their dark combat clothes blended perfectly into the woodland floor. The boots of a UNIT patrol passed by within inches of them. Once it had moved away they got up. Slowly, they began to work their way towards the house. They moved in utter silence – just like ghosts.

Jo said indignantly, 'Sergeant Benton! You took years off my life, creeping about like that.'

'Didn't want to disturb the Doctor. What's he up to anyway?'

'Nothing very much. He's either tinkering with that black box you found, or carrying on like a one man Wine and Cheese society!'

At the mention of food and drink Benton cheered up. He was a big chap, and he needed a lot of fuel to keep him going. He leaned forward confidentially. 'Couldn't spare me a bite, could you, Miss Grant? I'm famished.' He did his best to look undernourished.

Jo said, 'You wait here.' She marched back into the study.

The Doctor had cut himself another piece of Stilton and poured out another glass of wine. He was contemplating them with anticipation when Jo entered and took both plate and glass from his hand.

'Jo!' he said protestingly.

'All in a good cause, Doctor.'

The Doctor watched her disappear through the door. He sighed, and reached for the cheese knife.

Benton beamed as Jo put the plate and glass on a hall table beside him. 'You've saved my life, Miss.'

He was just reaching out when a familiar voice said, 'And what do you think you're doing, Sergeant Benton?' Captain Yates stood in the main doorway.

Benton straightened up to attention and saluted. 'Just checking up, sir.'

'I see, Sergeant. Then perhaps you'd like to check up on number two patrol?'

Benton said, 'Yessir.' With an anguished glance at the little table, he disappeared into the darkness.

Mike Yates seemed to notice the plate and glass for the first time. 'Why, Jo, how very kind of you!' He swigged down the wine and popped a piece of cheese into his mouth.

Jo looked at him severely. 'Mike Yates, that was mean.'

'R.H.I.P.,' said Mike indistinctly, his mouth full of cheese.

Jo looked at him blankly. 'Come again?'

'R.H.I.P.,' he repeated. 'Rank Has Its Privileges.' He gave her a smile, and followed Benton out into the night. Jo went back to the study.

The Doctor looked up. 'So what was all *that* about?'

'Oh nothing. Just feeding the troops.'

The Doctor nodded approvingly. 'Quite right. I remember saying to old Napoleon, you know, Boney, I said, always remember this… an army marches on its stomach.'

Jo sniffed. 'Well Mike Yates certainly does.' A gust of wind rattled the window panes and she looked up nervously. 'Doctor, did you mean what you said to the Brigadier about ghosts?'

The Doctor smiled. 'I also said there were different kinds of ghosts.'

'I know, ghosts from the past, and ghosts from the future. Which kind did you have in mind?'

The Doctor looked at her seriously. 'Isn't it far more a question of whether they have us in mind?'

By now the guerillas were very close to the house. They had concealed themselves in a clump of bushes close to the study window. Boaz said, 'In there. He must be in there. Come on.' He was about to move forward, when a UNIT patrol crunched along the gravel path. Boaz pulled himself down into cover again.

Another gust of wind rattled the study windows, and rain lashed against the panes. The Doctor crossed to the French windows and pulled back the heavy curtains. 'It's certainly a wild night, Jo. I don't envy those poor chaps on patrol.' He stood for a moment looking out into the blackness.

*

In the clump of bushes Boaz raised his gun and took aim. The tall figure in the window made a perfect target.

Suddenly his arm was pushed aside. He looked angrily at Anat.

'For heaven's sake, Anat,' he hissed, 'it's him, the man we came to kill! One shot and it's all over.'

'No,' Anat said fiercely. 'We must be sure. We'll go inside the house.'

'Too late now, anyway,' said Boaz sourly. The figure had left the window.

Anat said, 'We'll wait a moment longer. Then we go in.'

Inside the study Jo said, 'I never got that cup of tea!' Once more she set off for the kitchen.

The Doctor picked up the black box, and began to examine it for the hundredth time. Restlessly he turned it over and over in his long fingers.

He slipped off the back and began to peer at the maze of alien circuitry inside.

'Thing's a complete botch-up,' he grumbled to himself. 'Shouldn't work at all, but it does. Or did. Must be a booster somewhere or you wouldn't get the power.' Muttering to himself he bent absorbedly over the little box.

At a signal from Anat the three guerillas burst from the bushes. They knew that their moment of greatest danger would come in crossing the little patch of open ground between the bushes and the house itself. Just as they were completely in the open a two-man UNIT patrol rounded

51

the corner of the house.

For a split second the soldiers peered at the dim figures before them. One of the soldiers snapped, 'Who goes there? Give the password.'

When there was no answer the UNIT men raised their guns. But Boaz and Shura were already shooting. There was a high-pitched electronic buzz, and the UNIT patrol vanished, totally disintegrated.

Anat gave an anguished look at her two fellow guerillas. But she knew there had been nothing else for them to do. This mission had to succeed, even at the cost of innocent lives. She gave Shura a quick signal. He moved to the French windows. Anat and Boaz slipped through the front door of the house.

In the study, the Doctor gave up the time machine in disgust. Nothing he could do seemed to make it come to life again. He slammed it down on the table. Immediately, it began to give out a low hum, and the swirling shimmering effect appeared very faintly around it.

The Doctor looked at the device in amazement. 'Hey, Jo,' he called. 'I've got it working again. Come and see. Jo, where are you?'

Jo heard the Doctor calling her from the kitchen, though she couldn't hear what he was saying. Still, it might be urgent. She abandoned her tea-making and headed back to the study.

Shura peered through the gap in the curtains. To his utter

amazement he saw a time machine standing on the table. And it was operational! The one thing that was certain to bring the Daleks and their Ogron killers down upon them.

Shura crashed his booted foot against the lock of the French windows. They flew open, and he shot into the room amid a shower of glass.

The tall man had been standing in the doorway, but he whirled round with amazing speed at Shura's entrance.

Shura had temporarily forgotten that he had come to kill this man. He only wanted him to turn off the time transmitter before the Daleks picked up the signal. But before he could even speak an amazingly long leg shot out and kicked the gun from his hand. Shura dived desperately for the time machine. But the tall man obviously mistook this for an attack.

He dodged, reached out, and Shura found himself gripped by long steely fingers. Somehow he was spun, twisted and sent crashing into the wall. He slid to the floor half dazed. The one thought in his mind was that the man must, *must* be made to turn off the time transmitter, which still pulsed away.

In the Temporal Scanning Room the Controller of Earth Sector One peered eagerly at the screen. The tiny pulse was very faint. He turned to the girl technician beside him. 'This time, you *must* fix the co-ordinates.'

'We are attempting to do so now, Controller!' A panel in the far wall slid open. A squat, black metallic figure glided towards them. Its eye-stalk swung round onto the

Controller, and the harsh, metallic voice grated, 'What is happening? Report.'

The Controller said, 'We have located a time transmitter operating in the twentieth century zone. We're fixing the co-ordinates now.' He shot a quick look at the impassive girl technician beside him and hoped desperately that his words were true. Hastily he went on, 'Security patrol are standing by.'

The Black Dalek swivelled round, turning its eye-stalk towards the faint pulse on the screen. The Dalek voice rasped: 'Whoever is operating the time transmitter is an enemy of the Daleks. They are to be exterminated.' Once again the voice rose almost to a shriek. 'Exterminate them! EXTERMINATE THEM! EXTERMINATE THEM!'

In Sir Reginald Styles' study, Shura struggled desperately to his feet. He pointed to the pulsating time transmitter and croaked, 'Please turn it off. You must turn it off or they'll kill us all!'

The tall man hauled Shura to his feet and dumped him down in an armchair. 'To be quite honest I don't think I *can* turn it off. I'm not even very sure how I turned it on. Now then, my friend, I want to ask you one or two questions.'

From the doorway a girl's voice said: 'Get away from him.'

The Doctor turned from his captive. He saw a thin, dark girl in guerilla costume. Next to her another guerilla, a man. He had Jo Grant held firmly in front of him, a gun at her head.

Obediently the Doctor moved away. The girl went straight to the time machine, and with a few complex manipulations of the controls managed to turn it off.

In the Temporal Scanning Room, the Controller's heart sank as he looked at the blank screen. He turned to the girl technician, hoping against hope... Perhaps there had still been time to trace the transmission.

The usually impassive technician's voice held a tremor of fear as she said, 'I'm sorry. We've lost the trace.'

The Black Dalek swung round on her angrily. Then it swung back to the Controller. The Dalek gun was pointing straight at him. The Controller knew that he might well be blasted into extinction then and there. The Daleks had no mercy on those who failed them. He stood perfectly still, not daring to breathe, trying not to even think. There was a long and terrible silence. Then the Black Dalek turned and glided out of sight.

5

Condemned to Death!

With an air of grim satisfaction the guerillas surveyed their prisoners.

Jo stood motionless, still held by Boaz, who had grabbed her in the hall. The Doctor leaned his shoulders against the mantelpiece and looked round the room. He appeared utterly calm and relaxed, yet Jo could see that his eyes were bright and alert, his long thin body poised for instant action.

The Doctor nodded towards Boaz and said mildly, 'I think you might let the young lady go. She's scarcely likely to harm you.'

Boaz suddenly felt rather foolish holding his gun to the head of such a very small girl. He let her go. She gave him an indignant glare and walked across to the Doctor.

Ignoring Jo completely, Anat walked towards the Doctor, gun in hand. She looked up into his face. 'So you're the man. Outwardly so innocent looking, yet capable of such terrible crimes. Who would ever know?'

The Doctor gave her a puzzled look. 'I'm sorry, young lady, but I haven't the faintest idea what you're talking about.'

Anat snapped: 'Silence! You have done enough talking. It is time for your execution.'

Jo looked at the girl appalled. Why would anyone want to execute the Doctor? She felt the girl was working herself up into a kind of frenzy – as though she couldn't quite face the idea of killing in cold blood.

The same thought had occurred to the Doctor. The girl wasn't a natural killer, but she had it within her to shoot him down in certain circumstances. In a deliberate attempt to lower the emotional temperature he said, 'Execution? Don't I even get a trial?'

Anat said, 'We have our orders.'

'No doubt. But whose orders?'

'That does not concern you.' Anat stepped back. 'Boaz, Shura!'

All three guerillas trained their guns on the Doctor. Desperately, Jo threw herself in front of him. 'Please, leave him alone. He's never done anyone any harm.'

Gently, the Doctor took Jo by the shoulders and moved her out of danger. Then quite undisturbed by the three gun muzzles pointed at him he said, 'Young lady, may I say one thing?'

'A last-minute speech of repentance?' said Anat contemptuously.

'Not exactly. You see, I rather think you're making one terrible mistake.'

'And that is?'

'A simple question of identity. You think I'm Sir Reginald Styles, I imagine?'

'Of course you're Styles.'

'Ah, but that's the mistake you see. I'm not Styles at all.'

Anat looked at him scornfully. 'Very feeble, Sir Reginald. Is that the best you can do? You answer Styles' description. You're in his house.' She indicated the tray. 'You drink his wine and eat his food. But you're not Styles.'

Once again the three guerillas raised their guns. Jo was frozen with horror. She remembered the dummy she had made, the way it had shimmered and vanished. She tried to rush forward again, but Boaz caught her and threw her into an armchair, holding her down with his free hand.

'I admit that it does all sound a little implausible,' said the Doctor calmly, 'but perhaps you'd care to look at the newspaper on that table.'

Anat moved to the table and picked up the newspaper. It was last night's evening paper. The headline read 'STYLES

FLIES TO PEKING IN TALKS CRISIS'. 'There's even a picture of him,' said the Doctor cheerfully. 'As you can see we're not really very alike.'

Worried, Anat looked at the headline, the picture of Styles and then back at the Doctor. 'If you're not Styles – why are you here?'

'Believe it or not I was waiting for you.'

Boaz, who had been listening with increasing impatience, raised his gun. 'We're wasting time, Anat. Here, I'll do it.'

Anat knocked the gun aside with surprising force. 'I command this mission. We are soldiers, not murderers. Now get outside, I want you to keep guard.'

For a moment Boaz didn't move. Then he nodded and moved to the door.

Anat turned back to the Doctor. 'Now then, suppose you answer my question sensibly. How could you be waiting for me? You couldn't have known we were coming.'

'Oh but I did. You tried to kill Styles once. It was logical to assume you'd try again.'

'And you deliberately took his place? Why?'

'Because I wanted to talk to you. To discover *why* you want to kill Styles. To find out where you came from, and equally important – *when*.'

Anat looked up sharply. That last remark showed familiarity with the idea of time travel. Suddenly Boaz burst into the room. 'Soldiers! Coming up the path.'

Anat said, 'We must hide. Bring them!' and she pointed to the Doctor and Jo.

Quickly the guerillas hustled their captives out into the

hall. The crunch of army boots could be heard coming up the path. Anat looked round. There was a big, wooden door beneath the staircase and a flight of steps leading downwards. 'Down there,' she ordered.

Pushed by the three guerillas, Jo and the Doctor stumbled downwards into the darkness. They heard Anat hiss, 'You are both covered by our guns. One sound and you will be dead.' The little group huddled silently in the darkness.

Sergeant Benton and his patrol looked round the empty hallway. He called, 'Doctor! Jo! Where are you?' There was no reply.

Benton said to the soldiers: 'Take a look in the other rooms.' The soldiers clattered off, scattering through the house.

Benton spotted the door under the stairs and pushed it open. He found a light switch and pressed it. A single grimy bulb illuminated a flight of wooden steps leading down to a whitewashed cellar. Row upon row of wine racks stretched away into the darkness. Benton yelled: 'Anyone down there?' There was no answer.

Only a matter of inches away from him a silent group crouched behind the massive cellar door. Jo and the Doctor could feel the cold metal of guns pressing against their foreheads. Benton paused uneasily... something didn't feel right... Then he heard Captain Yates calling him. He turned out the light and closed the cellar door.

Yates was standing in the hallway, his face grave. 'Number two patrol failed to report in, Sergeant Benton. They seem to have vanished.'

Benton said, 'So has the Doctor, sir. And Miss Grant. Study window's smashed open, and there seems to have been a struggle. You reckon they've been kidnapped?'

The soldiers came back into the hall. One of them said, 'We've checked every room, Sarge. Whole place is empty.'

Yates looked at his watch. 'It'll be light before long. We'll make a full-scale search of the ground and check with all the other patrols. Someone must have seen something.' He turned and led the way out of the house.

When the noise of the soldiers' departure had faded away, Anat pressed the light switch again. She looked down the steps into the cellar and said, 'This will do for the moment. Tie them up and gag them!'

Boaz and Shura shoved the Doctor and Jo down the steps. Anat went out into the hall, back into the study and peered cautiously out of the window. Dawn was very near now. There were already pale streaks of light in the east. Dimly, Anat could see the woods and lawns of Austerly Park. She gazed at the peaceful landscape with a kind of wonder. Then she looked around the study; for the first time she realised that she had actually journeyed into the past. The comfort and luxury of old houses, well-furnished rooms such as this, had long been things of the past when Anat was born. She reached out and touched the softness of the velvet curtains.

The entrance of Boaz and Shura recalled her to the realities of her mission. They were not here to enjoy Earth's past, but to change its future.

Boaz said, 'They'll be no trouble for a while.' He turned

to Anat with a hint of challenge in his voice. 'Well, what happens now?'

'I'm going to ask for fresh orders. The whole situation has changed.' She produced the little sub-temporal voice transmitter from her tunic and spoke into it. '*Mission intercept to base... mission intercept to base...*' There came only a crackling. Anat shook her head, 'It's no good. There's some kind of disturbance in the Time Vortex.'

Shura said, 'Why don't I go back to the tunnel, Anat? The big booster transmitter's there. That'll get through.'

Anat thought for a moment. 'All right. Tell them what's happened. Ask them for a prediction on Styles. They may be able to look up the date of his return here. Now hurry, it'll be light soon.'

Shura slipped out of the French windows and faded away into the darkness.

Anat sank into a chair, realising for the first time how tired she was. Boaz looked down at her and said, 'Surely it's obvious what we should do?'

'Is it?'

'We're *here* now. Actually in Styles' house. We wait till he returns and then kill him.'

Anat looked at him wearily. 'And suppose Styles *doesn't* return? How long do you think we can stay here undetected? What about those two down in the cellar?'

'They might come in useful as hostages.'

'And if they don't? If they become a danger to us?'

Boaz shrugged. 'Then we kill them.'

*

Down in the cellar the Doctor was wiggling his neck and chin in the most amazing manner. With a last desperate twist, he managed to free the gag from his mouth and chin. 'Ah, that's better,' he exclaimed with a sigh of relief.

'Mmmmm,' said Jo indignantly. 'Mmm mmmm mmmmm mm?'

The Doctor regarded her thoughtfully. 'I'm not at all sure I shouldn't leave you like that. It's very peaceful.'

There came a fresh outburst of indignant 'mmm's from Jo, and the Doctor rolled over to her. After a bit more effort he managed to pull her gag away with his teeth.

Immediately Jo burst out, 'Doctor! Who are these people? Why do they want to kill Styles? Where do they come from?'

The Doctor said, 'One thing at a time, Jo. And it's not where, but *when*. In terms of technological progress, I'd say they're about two hundred years ahead of your time.'

'The twenty-second century?' said Jo.

'Visiting the twentieth,' said the Doctor thoughtfully, 'on a special mission through time to find a certain politician and kill him. But why?'

'You're the one with the answers, Doctor.'

'Well, for a start, they're not criminals.'

'Oh aren't they?' said Jo indignantly. 'They were going to murder you, remember.'

'The word they used was "execute". They're political fanatics. I think they've come here to try and change history. And that's a very fanatical idea.'

The Doctor was quiet for a moment, then he said, 'Let

me have a go at getting your ropes off, Jo. At least it'll help to pass the time.'

The Controller stood watching as Dalek scientists supervised the installation of a massive and complex piece of equipment in the Temporal Scanning Room. He turned and spoke to the Black Dalek at his side. 'We are maintaining a constant watch upon the Time Vortex. If we detect a transmission that continues long enough and strong enough, we shall certainly be able to trace it to its source.'

The Black Dalek intoned, 'All enemies of the Daleks must be tracked down and destroyed.'

The Controller said, 'This new equipment... I am not quite clear as to its purpose.'

'Since you are unable to capture the criminals unaided, the science of the Daleks will help you. This is the Magnetron. If the time transmitter that was traced is used again, anyone so doing will be diverted in the Space Time Vortex and materialise here.'

'But only if that particular machine is used?'

'It is necessary to set the Magnetron to the frequency of a particular transmitter.' The Black Dalek's answer sounded almost sulky.

The Controller wasn't very impressed. *If* one particular time machine was used they *might* be able to capture the person using it. Since the resistance fighters knew that all transmissions risked being traced, it was highly unlikely that the machine would be used again. But the Controller knew better than to express his doubts. Humbly he bowed his head.

The Black Dalek said, 'It is likely that the criminals will have returned to the spatial co-ordinates where the first criminal was located. You will despatch another security patrol to that place and time zone.'

The Controller looked up sharply.

'With respect, is that wise?' he asked. 'If they are seen…'

The Dalek rounded on him fiercely, its voice rising to a pitch almost of hysteria: 'Do not dispute with the Daleks! The function of the human is to obey!'

Again the Controller bowed his head, and followed the Black Dalek from the room. The Daleks were becoming frightened, he thought. Fear could have only one result – to make them even more ruthless than before. And that meant harshness and oppression for Earth. As he followed the Black Dalek along the endless corridors of Central Control his mind was busy.

What were the resistance guerillas up to in the twentieth century time zone? What did they hope to achieve that the Daleks were so desperate to prevent? The Controller entered his office and gave the orders that would despatch a patrol of Ogrons back to the railway tunnel where the first guerilla had been found.

It took Shura a long time to reach the tunnel. He was helped by the fact that he was alone instead of one of a group of three. But it was beginning to get light now, and the grounds were alive with searching UNIT troops.

For a long time Shura hid in a tree near the outer

wall. When at last the patrols had finished searching that particular area he dropped down from his tree and began to scale the wall. At the last moment he was spotted. He heard a shout of alarm as he dropped down on the other side of the wall and sprinted for the tunnel. He guessed the soldiers would follow him.

Once inside he paused to get used to the darkness. He fumbled his way along to the hidden cavity where he had stowed their equipment. Moving aside the two heavy Dalekenium bombs, he fished out the big transmitter, and started to use it. '*Mission intercept to base… mission intercept to base…*'

But even the powerful main transmitter picked up only crackling and static. There was obviously some kind of massive disturbance in the Space Time Vortex, thought Shura. Maybe some new invention of the Daleks. Their time travel technology was constantly improving.

He was about to try again when a massive booted foot stamped down on the transmitter, smashing it beyond repair. Shura looked up to see an Ogron grinning savagely down at him. The Ogron hauled him to his feet, and smashed him against the tunnel wall. His gun was ripped from his holster, before he could use it.

Shura was young and strong, and he fought desperately. But like any human being he was helpless against an Ogron's strength. The Ogron gripped him in a savage bear hug, then hurled him to the ground. As he tried to rise a booted foot smashed him savagely in the ribs. He rolled away desperately as the Ogron kicked again.

Shura had one advantage in the unequal struggle. He guessed that the Ogron didn't want to kill him. Or rather it wanted to, but had been ordered instead to take him alive. The beating-up was merely a way of relieving its frustrations at being deprived of the pleasure of destroying him. Shura rolled towards the cavity and groped inside. Next to the bombs was a spare disintegrator pistol. As the Ogron reached for him again Shura rolled and came up with the gun in his hands. He fired, and the Ogron was blasted into nothingness.

Shura sank down against the side of the tunnel wall, gasping for breath. He took stock of his injuries: several ribs were broken for sure, and one arm. There must be other Ogrons about, he thought muzzily. He wouldn't survive long if they found him. There was only one possible hiding-place.

Scrabbling aside the rubble with his good hand, Shura enlarged the cavity they had used as a cache. He dug out a space big enough to lie in, pulled the ruined transmitter and the gun in after him, and then covered the supplies and himself with rubble.

Minutes later other Ogrons came lumbering along the tunnel. Shura heard shouts, and then shots. He heard the Ogrons muttering briefly in low guttural voices. Then there was the familiar hum of a time transmitter; Shura guessed that the Ogrons had been spotted by the UNIT troops, and were returning to their own time zone. Soon he heard more human shouts, and the sound of army boots.

Shura should have been found by the army patrol. But

the UNIT troops had already had one experience of chasing Ogrons into the tunnel and finding it empty. Perhaps, too, they weren't too keen to linger long in the tunnel, just in case those gorilla things *hadn't* all gone. In any case, the soldiers rushed in quickly one end and out the other.

Shura heard one of them call: 'No good, Corp, they've faded away again.' That shout was the last thing Shura heard for quite a while.

Battered and exhausted, suffering not only from his wounds but from the strain of the last few hours, he felt himself drift into a state of unconsciousness. Soon, curled up in his nest of rubble, bombs and pistol clasped to his chest, Shura was fast asleep.

Anat and Boaz waited for Shura's return with increasing unease. Both jumped when the telephone began to ring. Although neither had seen or used a telephone before, they knew well enough what it was.

They stared at it helplessly, wishing it would stop. But the ringing went on and on. Anat reached a hand out towards the 'phone. Boaz snapped: 'Leave it!'

'They'll be suspicious if no one answers,' said Anat desperately. She came to a decision. 'Those people in the cellar. Bring them up.'

Boaz dashed from the room, and Anat waited for what seemed an agonisingly long time. Still the telephone kept up its unending ringing and ringing.

Boaz came back into the room, herding Jo and the Doctor before him with his pistol. Anat said, 'Untie him.' Boaz cut the ropes from the Doctor's wrists and pushed him towards the 'phone. 'Answer it,' said Anat. 'Tell them everything's all right.' Boaz held the gun to the Doctor's head.

Slowly, the Doctor picked up the receiver and said 'Hello?'

'Sorry to bother you so early,' said the Brigadier. 'Been up all night with this conference crisis.'

'That's all right, Brigadier. As a matter of fact, I've been up all night myself.'

'Ghost-hunting, eh?' The Brigadier chuckled. 'Anything happen?'

Anat moved her head close to the Doctor's, so that she too could hear what the Brigadier was saying.

'Nothing happening,' responded the Doctor calmly. 'Everything's very quiet here.'

'Jolly good. Thing is I had some kind of garbled report from Yates and Benton that you'd vanished. They looked in the house and couldn't find you. Said the place was deserted.'

The Doctor said, 'Did they? Oh yes, must have been when we were down in the cellar. Did I tell you old Styles has a fascinating collection of wines?'

'Now listen, Doctor, you're absolutely sure everything's all right at that house? Because Styles is coming back there tomorrow night. He is taking the main delegates to his house for an informal preliminary conference.'

Boaz and Anat exchanged exultant glances. Before anyone could stop him the Doctor said, 'I'm not sure that's wise, Brigadier.'

Boaz, thrust the gun closer to the Doctor's head. Anat gave him a look of warning.

'Oh really? Why not?'

The Doctor didn't reply.

After a moment the Brigadier said, 'You're sure everything *is* all right, Doctor?'

Speaking clearly and distinctly the Doctor said, 'I assure you, Brigadier, there's nothing to worry about. Tell Styles that. Tell the Prime Minister. And, Brigadier, be particularly sure to tell it to the Marines.' Hoping that his knowledge of twentieth century slang was accurate, the Doctor put down the 'phone.

At UNIT H.Q., the Brigadier turned to Yates and Benton. 'You were right. The Doctor's in trouble. I think he's been made prisoner. We're going back to Austerly House right away.' He paused at the door. 'Oh, and send a message to the patrols. They're to keep the house surrounded, but they're not to go inside.'

Anat and Boaz were jubilant. 'He's coming here!' exclaimed Anat. 'Sir Reginald Styles is coming here! We can carry out our mission.'

'Of course,' said Boaz, 'the conference *is* here tomorrow night. Our dates were right after all.'

'You certainly showed a remarkable ability to predict the future,' agreed the Doctor, 'though I suppose it's not so remarkable really, since our future is your past.' Boaz and Anat were scarcely listening to him.

Nor was Jo. Before the guerillas had brought them up from the cellar, she and the Doctor had practically succeeded in getting the ropes off her wrists. Although the Doctor's wrists had been tied he had still been able to use his fingers, and by standing back to back he had been able to untie most of the knot. Now Jo was finishing the job herself. Suddenly, she was free. And no one seemed to be worrying about her.

The Doctor made a second attempt to talk to Anat. 'Isn't it about time you told me what you think you're up to? Why do you imagine that killing Styles will make any difference to the future you come from?'

Anat said, 'It will make every difference.'

'Styles isn't a bad man… At the moment he's doing all he can to stop a world war…'

'You believe that?' said Anat. 'You really believe that?'

'Most certainly.'

'Then I've got some rather startling news for *you*. Your friend Styles isn't trying to stop a war – he's going to start one… unless we can stop him.'

Jo dashed across the room and picked up the time machine. She raised it threateningly above her head.

'Right,' she snapped, 'you can both drop your guns.'

Anat and Boaz made no move to obey her.

'If you don't do as I say,' said Jo determinedly, 'I'm going to smash this machine to bits. You'll be stranded here for ever. You'll never get back to your own time.'

The Doctor said, 'Jo, you've got it all wrong… Put that machine down before it starts working again.'

Jo ignored him. Looking at Boaz and Anat she said, 'I

warn you, I mean it.'

Anat sounded almost sorry for her. 'My dear child, we don't need that machine. We have others of our own.'

Jo looked at her uncertainly. 'You're just bluffing.'

'I assure you I'm not,' said Anat. 'Now put that machine down and stop being silly.'

To Jo's amazement the Doctor said, 'Jo, do as she says.'

Confused, Jo gripped the machine tighter. Unconsciously her fingers tightened over the control knobs. Suddenly the machine hummed into life. A shimmering effect filled the air around Jo's body. She felt herself in the grip of some terrible force, drawing her away... and before the Doctor's horrified gaze, Jo, still clutching the time machine, just faded and vanished away...

6

Prisoner of the Daleks

Jo Grant was twisting and turning in a sort of strange misty nothingness. Soon she lost all sense of up or down. Over and over, round and round she went. All the time she could feel the tug of powerful forces that seemed to be pulling her apart. She felt sick and dizzy and terrified. Just when she could bear it no longer all the different pulls seemed to combine. She felt herself being drawn steadily in one particular direction.

Gradually it seemed that she was becoming more solid, more real... the misty nothingness was fading away... she was in a real place again... she could feel a solid floor beneath her. It was cold and metallic.

Cautiously, Jo opened her eyes and looked around her. She was in some kind of control room, surrounded with gleaming alien machinery. Towering above her was a group of huge, ape-like creatures with savage cruel faces. They carried guns, big pistols like those used by the guerillas. The guns were all pointing straight at her.

The Doctor called: 'Jo! Jo!' but it was too late. She had completely vanished. He turned to Anat. 'What's happened to her?'

Anat's look was almost sympathetic. 'The machine was faulty. She's probably been disintegrated, dispersed for ever into the Time Vortex.'

Boaz said, 'That's if she was lucky.'

'And if she wasn't?' said the Doctor grimly.

Again the look of sympathy from Anat. 'If the machine was still working, it's possible that she'll be re-embodied in our time.'

'Believe me,' Boaz added ominously, 'she'd be better off dead.' He indicated the Doctor with his pistol. 'What do we do with him?'

'Put him back in the cellar. Tie him up again.'

While Anat covered him with her gun, Boaz put the ropes back on the Doctor's wrists. The knots were cruelly tight. No chance of undoing them again, thought the Doctor.

When the binding was finished Boaz stepped back. 'All right, get moving.' The Doctor ignored him, and looked at Anat. 'There's nothing you can do to save my friend? Nothing at all?'

Anat shook her head. 'Believe me, I'm sorry. But she brought it on herself. We didn't want to harm anyone unnecessarily.'

Boaz came up to the Doctor and jabbed the gun in his ribs. 'Now listen, you! Anat may be soft-hearted but I'm not. As far as I'm concerned you're just a nuisance, and I'd as soon kill you. Now get back to that cellar.'

It was obvious that Boaz meant what he said. The Doctor went out of the study and into the hall. Boaz opened the cellar door, and shoved him down the steps.

The Doctor lay in darkness on the cold stone floor. For a moment a wave of despair washed over him. At the moment it seemed that the guerillas might well succeed in their plan to kill Styles and start another war, though why should they want to do that? The Doctor sighed. And now Jo was gone, perhaps dead, perhaps stranded in some alien and terrifying future.

It wasn't in the Doctor's nature to give up for very long. Surely the Brigadier had understood his message? Anyway, the one thing you could always do was try. Patiently the Doctor began to work on the ropes that bound his wrists.

Guarded by two of the ape-like monsters, Jo Grant was being marched along a series of endless, gleaming metal corridors. From time to time they passed shabbily dressed men and women bustling about on mysterious tasks. The place was like an anthill, thought Jo. Everyone seemed cowed and terrified, standing aside rapidly, and showing no curiosity at the sight of Jo.

They reached a sort of office, and Jo was thrust into a chair. Behind a desk sat a thin, dark man with a haggard, haunted face.

The two monsters took up a position behind Jo's chair. The man waved them away. 'You can go now.' For a moment they didn't move. The man said again, 'Go!' They turned and lumbered from the room.

The man smiled at Jo. 'They're only servants, you see. And so stupid! Nothing to be frightened of really.'

Jo said, 'What are they?'

'A kind of higher anthropoid. They used to live in scattered communities on one of the outer planets. They make useful servants.'

For a moment Jo had a ridiculous picture of one of the hulking gorilla-things coming in with a tea-tray. She giggled. 'Servants? What do they do?' she asked.

'We use them as a kind of policeman, or rather to help the police.'

'I see,' said Jo brightly. 'You mean they're sort of police dogs?'

'Exactly. They are very faithful, very loyal.'

Jo was beginning to feel less frightened. The explanation did make the creatures less terrifying. After all people had used guard dogs for ages, and it was the same thing really. And the man seemed to be friendly enough.

'Look, I know it sounds silly, but could you please tell me where I am?' she said.

'You're at Central Control in Sector One. In fact, I'm the Controller of the Region.' There was pride in the man's voice. His rank was obviously important to him.

'Yes, but where? What planet?'

The man seemed puzzled. 'Why, Earth of course. Where else?'

'But it's all so different,' said Jo helplessly.

'That's because you've travelled in time. You see, this is the twenty-second century.'

For a moment Jo's head reeled. The Controller said reassuringly, 'Don't worry. We can get you back to your own time. Is that what you want?'

Jo nodded eagerly. 'Yes, of course.'

The Controller sat back in his chair, 'First I'd like you to tell me everything that happened to you before you found yourself here.'

The Controller sat back and listened as the girl told her story. He congratulated himself on his handling of the situation. It had been obvious from the start that the girl was no guerilla. But her possession of the time machine meant she must have been in contact with them, probably quite innocently. And her story was bearing out his theory.

When Jo had finished, the Controller sat back for a moment, trying to digest the flood of new information. He wished his knowledge of twentieth century history were better. What was so important about this man Styles?

Jo said, 'The really worrying thing is, the Doctor is still their prisoner.'

Her heart sank as the Controller said solemnly, 'I'm afraid your friend is in very great danger.'

'But why? They know now he's the wrong man.'

The Controller's face was grave. 'You don't know these people as I do, Miss Grant. I've spent years trying to track them down. They've been responsible for the most terrible crimes. And if anyone gets in their way, they're totally without mercy.'

Jo remembered the burning fanatical eyes of the three guerillas. She shuddered. 'I can well believe it,' she said.

The Controller leaned forward across his desk. 'Now, we may be able to mount a rescue operation to save this friend of yours. But we'll need your help.'

'Yes, of course. Anything at all.'

'We know where these criminals are holding your friend. We have maps that show where Austerly House once stood. But equally important is the "*when*". Can you remember exactly what time they arrived?'

Jo nodded. 'Just after midnight.'

'Yes, but the date, the month, the year?'

Puzzled, Jo told him. The Controller gave a sigh of relief. 'Excellent. I'm sure we'll be able to help your friend. Now I must ask you to excuse me. I must start arranging the rescue expedition at once.'

'And you'll take me with you, get me back to my own time?'

The Controller came from behind his desk and took Jo's arm.

'Naturally, naturally. Now I'm sure you're tired, hungry and thirsty. We have special refreshment suites for honoured guests. Let me take you to one…'

He paused at the door. 'When the criminals transferred to your time, did they arrive near the house itself?'

'I doubt it,' said Jo. 'The UNIT guards would have seen them.'

'Have you any idea where they did arrive? Some kind of hideout in your time, perhaps?'

Jo frowned. 'There's an old railway tunnel near the house. That's where we found the wounded man, and the time machine. They could have hidden in there. It's a very long tunnel, and completely abandoned.'

'A tunnel?' said the Controller. 'Excellent. Now come

with me. I'll let you know as soon as there's any news.'

A few minutes later, the Controller stood once more before the Black Dalek.

'I have won her trust completely. Thanks to me we now have the information we need.'

The Controller knew that there would be no word of praise for his success. Daleks spoke only to condemn failure. Their servants were expected to succeed, or pay the penalty.

The Black Dalek said, 'The criminals are using the tunnel as a transfer point. We will prepare an ambush in the twentieth century time zone.'

'Security forces are standing by,' the Controller said quickly. 'If you wish I will take charge of things myself.'

The Black Dalek swivelled its eye-stalk towards him. With a tinge of contempt in the guttural voice it said, 'This expedition is too important to be entrusted to a human. Some of us will accompany you. *The expedition will be led by the Daleks!*'

7

Attack of the Ogrons

Boaz looked out cautiously from behind the curtains. 'There are patrols all round the house, but they don't seem to be coming near it.'

Anat said, 'Well, why should they? They think the place is empty, apart from the Doctor and that poor girl.'

Boaz turned away from the window. 'They're bound to send people here before Styles comes back. I know from the history books – such a man will have many servants.'

Anat shrugged. 'It's a big house. We'll find somewhere to hide. In the attics perhaps, or down in the cellar with our prisoner.'

'Yes, of course,' said Boaz. 'Or we could take the servants hostage. We only need to survive until Styles arrives. Once we kill him, we either escape or die. Doesn't really matter which, does it?'

Anat looked at him with concern. She wondered how much longer Boaz would be able to stand the waiting. He could only bear it by screwing himself up to a pitch of fanatic dedication. Her own nature was calmer, more determined. She bitterly regretted the deaths they had caused – the girl, the UNIT patrol... But she accepted them as a necessary part of the price that must be paid if they were to succeed. In the same way she accepted that her own death might well be a part of that price.

Suddenly there came a familiar sound. They rushed to the window.

Ogrons were materialising outside the house. Boaz raised his gun and blasted the first one before it had time to get its bearings. Anat joined him at the window.

For a while it was a kind of grim target practice. An Ogron would materialise, look round, and be instantly shot down, vanishing as fast as it had arrived. But they couldn't get rid of them all. Others were materialising out of their line of fire and coming to join the attack.

The air was full of the savage buzzing of the disintegrator guns. Soon the rattle of machine-gun fire was added to the din.

Boaz said exultantly to Anat, 'It's the soldiers!'

UNIT patrols began to arrive, opening fire on the Ogrons. The soldiers tried to form a protective line in front of the house.

The UNIT soldiers fought at some disadvantage. The weapons of the Ogrons were far more effective. It took a full clip of machine-gun bullets to kill an Ogron. Anything less and the monsters just went on fighting, roaring with rage and pain, but hardly even slowed down. But one direct hit from an Ogron pistol could blast a UNIT soldier into extinction.

Boaz and Anat, shooting from the now shattered French windows, had disintegrator guns of their own, and the atomic power packs built into the handles were practically everlasting. But they were only two, and the Ogrons outnumbered them badly.

In the cellar the Doctor heard the sound of battle, and speeded up his attempt to escape. By flailing his legs about he had managed to upset a whole rack of wine bottles. They had fallen to the floor in a crash of broken glass. Now the Doctor was rubbing his bonds against the jagged end of a broken bottle.

A UNIT soldier blazed away at the nearest Ogron. Roaring, the creature sank slowly to the ground. The soldier reached for a new clip of bullets, but before he could fit it, another Ogron blasted him into oblivion at close range. The Ogron swung its gun onto another soldier, but Anat disintegrated it with a shot from the window.

Boaz yelled: 'The soldiers can't hold them!'

Anat saw that it was true. The UNIT forces had lost too many men. Before long the Ogrons would break through the protective cordon and get into the house. Anat saw that defeat was just a matter of time. 'We'll have to get back to the tunnel,' she shouted. She took a final shot at an Ogron and ran from the room.

Boaz waited a moment longer, firing from the window to cover her retreat. Then he too turned to go, only to find himself facing a very angry Doctor, covered with dust and cobwebs and bleeding from several cuts on the wrists.

Before Boaz could even speak the Doctor was upon him. A long arm reached out, and Boaz went hurtling across the room, his gun skidding across the floor before he had a chance to use it.

As the Doctor moved to pick up the gun a voice said: 'Keep still.' He felt the cold metal of a gun barrel on his neck. Anat was in the doorway. She said to Boaz, 'Out – get to the tunnel!' and he rushed from the room. Anat gave the Doctor a sudden shove, and turned to run after Boaz. As she did so there was a shattering crash and an Ogron burst through the French windows, smashing the few remaining panes of glass in the process.

At once the Doctor grappled with the Ogron, trying to get hold of its gun. The creature's strength was enormous, and the Doctor strove in vain to wrench the gun from the hairy paw; at the same time he fought to restrain the creature's other hand from grasping his throat. The Doctor knew he could never match the immense strength of his opponent. Instead he applied the judo principle of turning an enemy's strength against him. Giving way before the Ogron's rush, the Doctor rolled onto his back, shoved his feet into the Ogron's stomach and sent it flying. The top of the Ogron's head thudded into the wall. Plaster dropped from around holes in its surface, and the creature slid to the ground, stunned. The Doctor tried again to get its gun, but the weapon was still tightly gripped in the hairy paw. He remembered Boaz's dropped gun, scooped it up, and ran after the two guerillas.

The Doctor ran along the passages of the old house, through the kitchens and into a paved courtyard. He ran through a back gate and found himself on the gravel path at the rear of the house.

Quickly working out his bearings he decided to make for the tunnel. Something told him that his only hope of rescuing Jo was to stay with the guerillas. Two Ogrons ran round the corner of the house, cutting off his retreat. The Doctor raised Boaz's gun and fired. There was a buzz, and the Ogron exploded into nothingness. He turned the gun on the second Ogron, and fired again, but nothing happened. The thing was jammed, or empty. The Doctor hurled the gun at the monster's head, but missed. The Ogron grinned savagely, showing its yellow fangs. Slowly it raised its gun, enjoying the moment...

The Doctor braced himself, wondering what it would feel like to be disintegrated. There was the noise of an engine, and the Ogron turned to face a new enemy.

The Brigadier came roaring round the corner in a jeep. Before the Ogron could fire, the Brigadier drove straight into it, sending it flying through the air, then he slammed on the brakes.

As soon as the Ogron hit the ground it was up again, charging the jeep. Coolly, the Brigadier snatched up his Sterling from the seat beside him and emptied the full clip of bullets into the Ogron. Rocked back on its heels by the impact, the Ogron staggered, then slumped to the ground.

The Brigadier jumped down from the jeep, stepped over the Ogron's body, and walked up to the Doctor's grimy and bleeding figure.

'Are you all right, Doctor? What the blazes have you been up to?'

The Doctor gave him a weary grin. 'I'm fine – thanks to your most timely intervention.'

'Then perhaps you'll explain what's going on,' said the Brigadier sternly. 'What are these creatures?'

'I'll try to explain later,' said the Doctor. 'At the moment I'm in a bit of a hurry.' To the Brigadier's indignation, the Doctor jumped into the jeep and shot off.

'Come back, Doctor! Come back at once!' the Brigadier yelled. But the only response was a cheery wave as the jeep disappeared out of sight.

The Doctor sped through the grounds of Austerly House, and along the road that led to the tunnel. As he came in sight of it he saw Anat and Boaz running across the fields towards the tunnel mouth.

The Doctor took the jeep as close to the tunnel as he could. Then, abandoning it, he ran across the fields after the two guerillas.

Once inside the tunnel, he was in almost total darkness. He groped his way forward, cautiously. Ahead he could hear echoing footsteps. The footsteps stopped. A tiny point of light glowed in the distance. The Doctor made his way towards it.

A strange humming noise came from behind him and he turned round. In the darkness a kind of glowing circle had appeared from which was emitted an eerie light. Within the circle a shape began to form. It was a shape the Doctor knew only too well, that of his oldest and bitterest enemy. A Dalek was materialising in the tunnel!

In a moment the process was completed. Still glowing with the same sinister light the Dalek swivelled round its eye-stalk as if getting its bearings. The Doctor froze, flattening himself against the tunnel wall. Behind the Dalek, Ogrons were beginning to materialise.

As if it sensed the Doctor's presence the Dalek spoke. The familiar grating, metallic voice said, 'Stop! You are all enemies of the Daleks. Surrender, or you will be exterminated!' The Dalek began to trundle down the tunnel towards him.

8

A Fugitive in the Future

Again the Dalek voice echoed through the darkness of the tunnel, 'You are all enemies of the Daleks. Surrender at once or you will be exterminated!'

The Doctor realised the Dalek hadn't seen him at all. It was addressing the guerillas. Somehow it must know they were in the tunnel. He turned and ran on at full pelt through the darkness, towards the tiny glowing point of light.

As he got nearer he saw that the light came from a little torch-like device, held by Anat. She and Boaz stood side-by-side, hands joined. Each held a pulsating black box in the other hand. The two time-machines were pulsating rhythmically and already, the shimmering effect was beginning to build up.

As the Doctor ran up to them Anat screamed, 'Get back!'

Almost out of breath, the Doctor gasped, 'There's a Dalek... more Ogrons... in the tunnel behind me!'

The two guerillas turned. They saw the Dalek and the Ogrons bearing down on them. The Doctor pointed the other way. From that direction another Dalek, with Ogrons in support, was approaching. 'You're trapped,' said the Doctor.

The shimmering effect of the time field grew even stronger. Anat yelled, 'Get back! If you're caught up in the time field you'll be taken with us!'

The Doctor had no intention of being left behind... not with Daleks and Ogrons arriving from both sides. Instead of arguing, he wrapped his arms around Boaz in a determined bear-hug. The guerilla tried to break free, but the Doctor couldn't be budged. It became clear that wherever Boaz was going, the Doctor was going with him.

As their pursuers converged upon them, the little group shimmered and faded from sight. Like Jo Grant before him, the Doctor found himself twisting and twirling in the Time Vortex. Since he was used to time travel, he was much less frightened than Jo had been. He couldn't help thinking that time travel by this method was very different from time travel in the TARDIS. It was like comparing a trip in a luxury liner with going over Niagara Falls in a barrel.

Still holding grimly on to Boaz, the Doctor became aware that the Vortex was fading away. They were back in the real world. With a sudden jolt the Doctor found himself on firm ground. Letting go of Boaz, he looked round. They were still in a tunnel, but a very different one, more modern in design.

The two guerillas were checking equipment, and stowing away their time machines. Anat said, 'We warned you.'

The Doctor was looking around with interest. Only a single rail ran along this tunnel. They were in part of a monorail system. Probably built some time in the twenty-first century, and by now abandoned. Anat followed his glance. 'This may come as a shock to you,' she said gently, 'but you've travelled in time.'

The Doctor gave her a quizzical look. 'My dear young lady, I'm probably rather more familiar with time travel than you are.'

The guerillas started to move away. The Doctor said, 'Wait. Those Daleks we saw – where did they come from?'

Anat looked at him curiously. 'You know of the Daleks?'

'Indeed I do. You might say we're very old enemies. What are they doing on Earth in this time zone?'

Anat said flatly, 'They've ruled the Earth for almost two hundred years.'

'And if you knew about the Daleks you're a fool to have come here,' said Boaz.

'I came to find Jo Grant. As long as there's a chance that she's alive…'

Boaz said, 'Come, Anat, it's dangerous to stay here.'

'Please,' said the Doctor, 'how do I set about finding her?'

Boaz said, 'That's *your* problem!' He made another attempt to pull Anat away.

She hesitated. 'We can't just leave him to fend for himself.'

'I can,' said Boaz. 'Now, are you coming or not?'

Hurriedly Anat whispered to the Doctor, 'If the Daleks have got her she'll be at Central Control. But don't try to rescue her, it'd be suicide.'

Suddenly Boaz yelled, 'Run, Anat!' More Ogrons and Daleks were rushing at them out of the darkness.

The guerillas turned and ran. The Doctor ran too. This new set of tunnels was a complete maze, with openings in every direction. Here and there the tunnel roof was broken away so that patches of daylight lit up the gloom. The Doctor took a wrong turn and ran almost straight into an Ogron patrol! He turned and ran back with Ogrons pounding close behind him. As he turned into the opening of yet another tunnel, he saw a patch of light gleaming above him. In the half-light he looked around and saw some kind of hand-rail. The Doctor leaped for it and found himself hanging on to a maintenance ladder bolted to the wall. He clung there while the Ogrons ran past below him. Then, deciding that up was as good a direction as any, he started climbing the ladder.

It led up to a rusty trap-door. The Doctor managed to get his shoulder under it, and shoved hard. Reluctantly, the trap-door creaked open. Cautiously, the Doctor poked his head out, and wriggled through the trap-door into daylight.

All around him was a scene of complete and utter desolation. Every inch of the countryside, as far as he could see, seemed to have been built up till not an inch was left, then methodically hammered down. A sea of rubble stretched before him. Here and there a wall or two was still standing.

The Doctor fished a tiny instrument from his pocket. It was a sort of miniaturised Geiger counter. He tested the rubble around him. The little instrument began a subdued clicking.

The instrument was registering minute traces of

radioactivity. Atomic war had brought about this ruination. The radiation had faded as time went by.

The Doctor climbed a little hill of rubble and looked around him. In the distance a group of buildings stood out from the desolation. They were stark and ugly, made of rough concrete. They looked bleak, and functional, with nothing attractive or welcoming about them. They looked – there was only one word for it – 'Daleky'. The Doctor sighed. Unattractive as the buildings were, they made a point to aim for. There must still be people left on Earth. Perhaps someone would help him. He began to pick his way through the rubble.

The Controller of Earth Sector One was talking for his very life. After the latest failure to capture the guerillas, he had been summoned to appear before the High Council of the Daleks, the supreme ruling body of the planet Earth.

He stood, isolated in a pool of light, in a long, bare metallic room. It was completely featureless except for the raised area at the end. Here the dreaded Black Dalek and its superior, the even more powerful Golden Dalek, stood, with other Daleks grouped around them.

Briefly, the Controller ended his report. 'Security guards combed the tunnels, both here and in the twentieth century time zone. Nothing and no one was found. Our forces had to leave the twentieth century zone because of increased opposition from the human soldiers.'

For a moment there was silence. Then the Golden Dalek said, 'You have failed the Daleks. You will be punished.'

The Controller knew that appeals for mercy would be useless. He decided to speak his mind. At least he could die with dignity. 'Am I responsible for this failure? Ogron security guards carried out the mission. And was it not led by the Daleks themselves?' There was a stunned silence. Not for more than a hundred years had any human dared question the authority of the Daleks. The Controller went on, 'The Ogrons are stupid and clumsy! They are useless for operations of this kind. As guards in the work camps, perhaps... but definitely not for anything that calls for intelligence or initiative!'

There was a note of uncertainty in the voice of the Black Dalek. 'The Ogrons are loyal servants of the Daleks.'

'No doubt. But it takes humans to deal with humans. Now, if you would allow me to recruit *human* security guards...' (The Daleks used humans mostly for manual labour and simple administration.)

The Black Dalek said, 'Humans are treacherous and unreliable.'

'Not all humans,' replied the Controller, a little amazed at his own daring. 'I have served you loyally all my life.'

The Golden Dalek spoke again, 'Do not dispute with the Daleks. Obey without question. The hunt for the enemies of the Daleks must be carried on unceasingly. All enemies of the Daleks will be exterminated.'

The Controller sighed. He hadn't really expected any concessions. He was being turned away with the usual propaganda. At least he was still alive.

The Black Dalek said, 'Is your report concluded?'

'Except for one thing. It seems likely that a human returned from the twentieth century time zone with the guerillas. According to the patrols it must be the man the girl spoke about. She called him "the Doctor".'

He turned to leave. The Black Dalek's voice rose almost to a shriek –

'Stop! Doc-tor? Did you say, Doc-tor?'

The Controller was astonished at the strength of the reaction. The word 'Doctor' was pronounced jarringly in two syllables, and he could almost feel the hate in the Dalek's voice.

Now the Golden Dalek joined in, pronouncing the Doctor's name with the same venomous intensity. 'The one known as the Doc-tor is not human. He is the supreme enemy of the Daleks. He must be found and exterminated.'

Now the other Daleks took up the chorus. As the Controller left, their voices rang in his ears. 'Exterminate him! EXTERMINATE HIM! EXTERMINATE HIM!' But there was something different about those voices. They held some quality the Controller had never heard before, and as he walked from the council hall he recognised it. The quality was *fear*. For the first time in the Controller's experience of them the Daleks were actually afraid.

The Doctor had been travelling for many hours across the ruined landscape. Progress was slow. There were no roads to speak of, and the Doctor avoided those he saw. He had to be constantly alert for Ogron patrols, and always be ready to shelter in a ruin or a ditch. Once he had lain for what seemed ages in the cellar of a wrecked house while a resting Ogron patrol sat almost on top of him, chomping food from their pouches and talking in low guttural voices. At last they had moved on and he had been able to go on his way.

Now he had reached the edge of the enormous building which he had seen shortly after emerging from the trap-door. A high stone wall ran round it, with savage spikes at the top. Although the Doctor didn't know it a resistance leader called Moni had climbed that wall a few nights before. Looking for an easier way in, the Doctor moved along the wall cautiously. He passed what looked like a kind of lamp-post. But on top of it was not a lamp, but a monitor-lens. The Doctor unwittingly activated it when he passed through its field of vision. It swung round to follow him as he moved by.

On a screen somewhere inside the building a little spot of light began to move, recording the Doctor's progress. A girl technician leaned forward and spoke into a microphone. '*Alert, alert, intruder detected by outer wall. Description corresponds to that of wanted man known as "the Doctor".*'

'Allow him to enter the area, and then surround him. He must be captured alive.'

The Controller himself gave that final order. He knew the Daleks would probably prefer the Doctor to be killed on sight. But he was anxious to meet the man who could actually produce fear in the Daleks. He wasn't sure exactly why he felt like this. He only knew that he had to meet and talk to the Doctor before he let the Daleks dispose of him.

*

The Doctor meanwhile had found a small door in the wall. He was busy picking the simple electronic lock with the aid of his sonic screwdriver. Soon he had it open, and had slipped inside. He found himself inside a bare concrete yard which gave onto a number of barn-like buildings. Automated trucks on rails rumbled into them. The trucks were filled with crushed rock, obviously some kind of mineral ore.

He slipped across the courtyard and peered inside one of the long, low buildings. An endless conveyor belt ran right across it. Ragged, thin workers were standing beside the belt, sorting through the mineral ore with their bare hands. Others were staggering from the trucks to the belt with rock-filled baskets, keeping the conveyor supplied. The sorted-out ore moved off in another set of trucks, the rejected rocks were carried away and dumped onto another belt which took them out of sight. Ogron guards with whips stood by the workers. There was also a human guard who seemed to be in overall charge.

The Doctor watched the whole process with horror and indignation. The minerals arrived, were sorted, and were carried away. The whole process went on endlessly, and could obviously have been carried out entirely by machines. Probably the Daleks found it simpler and cheaper to wear out human beings instead, the Doctor thought angrily.

A thin old man stumbled and dropped his basket. Instantly, the human guard's whip cracked across his shoulders. The Doctor was quite unable to stop himself. He leaped from his cover, and next second the guard found himself flying through the air. He landed with a thump inside one of the trucks. The workers at the conveyer belt stopped working in astonishment. The Ogrons drew their guns.

Then a voice called, 'No!' It was the human chief guard climbing shakily out of the truck. 'The orders were to take him alive. And you needn't be gentle about it!'

Two Ogrons closed in on the Doctor. He ducked under the grip of one, and sent it spinning into its fellow. Both Ogrons fell. The Doctor sprinted for the door. Beside it stood two more Ogrons. They fell on him savagely, and within minutes the Doctor was beaten into unconsciousness. The Ogrons dragged him away. The human chief guard turned to the workers. 'Get on with your work – unless you want some of the same.' Hastily, they went back to their tasks, the Ogrons standing over them with their whips at the ready.

Moni slipped across the rubble and down the flight of stairs. It was dangerous to risk a daylight meeting, but the situation was urgent. As far as he knew this hideout was still secure. If Anat and the others had escaped...

He rapped out a complicated series of knocks on the door and to his relief the door was opened. Boaz was there, pale and weary. Beside him was Anat. Moni glanced round the cellar. 'Where's Shura?'

Anat said, 'We lost him. He went to contact H.Q., and never returned. They must have got him.'

Boaz said angrily, 'We were nearly caught getting back here ourselves.'

Moni listened silently while they told the story of the failure of their mission. He said, 'There's a girl being held prisoner at Central Control – she must be the one you're talking about. Can she tell them anything?'

Anat said, 'She knows we want to kill Styles. She can tell them that.'

Moni sighed wearily. Everything seemed to be going wrong. The mission had been a shambles from the start.

Anat asked, 'What about the man – the one who came back with us? Have they caught him yet?'

Moni shook his head. 'Not yet. But it's just a matter of time...'

9

Escape from the Ogrons

Jo Grant pushed her plate away with a sigh of pleasure. 'No more please. I couldn't eat another thing.'

The Controller leaned forward with a wine bottle. 'A little more wine?'

'No, honestly, nothing. It was a terrific meal.'

Actually, thought Jo, it hadn't been all that hot… coarse bread, tough meat and a mish-mash of strange vegetables. And she didn't think the Doctor would have thought much of the wine.

'I'm glad you enjoyed it,' he said. 'Few people eat so luxuriously these days.'

Jo thought he had a strange idea of luxury. She smiled, and said nothing. 'Nowadays,' the Controller went on, 'we have to get most of our main food elements from pills and tablets.'

The Controller sat back and smiled at her. 'Do go on telling me about your friend, the Doctor.'

'I don't think I can tell you anything more,' said Jo frankly. 'We've covered just about everything.' And indeed they had. The Controller seemed fascinated by the Doctor, and had asked question after question about him.

'You really don't know what he was doing *before* he joined this UNIT organisation?' asked the Controller.

'No idea,' said Jo firmly. 'No one knows very much about the Doctor, he's a very mysterious character. Look,' she went on hurriedly, 'please don't think I'm ungrateful, but you did say something about rescuing the Doctor, and getting me back to my own time.'

The Controller said, 'It isn't easy, you know. Our scientists are working on the problem.' He paused. 'As for your friend the Doctor, well, there's something I haven't told you. There's reason to believe that he followed you to this time zone.'

Jo was overjoyed. 'That's marvellous! Do you know where he is?'

'I'm afraid not. He was travelling with the criminals. No doubt they kidnapped him. We're carrying out a search for him at this very moment.'

A girl entered the room, bowed to the Controller and handed him a note. He waved in dismissal and she scuttled away. He opened the note, looked up at Jo and smiled. 'Good news, Miss Grant. Your friend the Doctor has been found. I'm going to fetch him now.'

Jo jumped up. 'Can I come with you?'

He shook his head. 'That isn't advisable. But don't worry, I assure you he's safe and well.'

At that particular moment the Doctor was in a bare metal cell, feeling on the very contrary both unsafe and unwell. He was at the end of a long and gruelling interrogation. The purpose seemed to be to get him to admit that he was in some kind of resistance movement. The guard hoped to impress his masters by producing a confession by the time they arrived. But despite some brutal handling the Doctor wasn't co-operating.

Again the guard yelled, 'Tell us who you are!'

'You'd never believe me,' said the Doctor wearily.

'Name your contacts in the criminal resistance movement.'

'Haven't got any.'

'What are you doing here?'

'Looking for a girl called Jo Grant. How many more times?'

'As many as it takes to get the truth out of you. Shall I hand you over to our friends here? They don't get much fun.' The guard indicated the two Ogrons holding the Doctor down in his chair.

The hairy paws were gripping his shoulders with brutal force.

'Poor fellows… that's too bad, but I'm not in the mood for games.'

The cell door opened and a small plumpish man entered. He wore plain dark clothing, with a civilian, rather than military look.

'Any progress?' he enquired.

The guard said, 'He's not being very co-operative.'

'How unwise of him. Perhaps I can persuade him. The rest of you wait outside.'

The guard looked rebellious for a moment. 'I said outside!' the newcomer repeated with an edge to his voice. At a nod from the guard the Ogrons released the Doctor and trooped out of the cell. The Doctor wriggled his aching shoulders. What next, he wondered.

The plump little man started to say, 'I am the manager of this work camp, and I advise you...' But as soon as the cell door closed behind the Ogrons, he changed his tone. He leaned close to the Doctor and hissed, 'Which group are you with?'

The Doctor sighed... 'Don't you start. I've just been telling your hairy friends... I'm not with any group.'

The manager's voice was frantic, 'You don't understand. I'm in the resistance myself. I want to help you. Now, who sent you here? What were you supposed to do?'

Angrily the Doctor said, 'Nobody sent me! I am *not* a spy *or* a guerilla. I'm simply trying to find...'

But the little man wasn't listening. As the cell door started to open he grabbed the astonished Doctor by the collar and did his best to shake him.

'You're a spy! Admit it, you're a spy!'

The new arrival entered the cell and said severely, 'Stop this at once! Why is this man being treated like this?' He turned to the Doctor and said, 'My dear Doctor, please permit me to apologise. I'm the Controller of this Sector. You're an elusive fellow, you know, I've had quite a job tracking you down.'

Gingerly, the Doctor rose to his feet. 'I'm glad you finally succeeded!'

By now he was beginning to feel that he must have broken into a madhouse.

'I've been looking forward to meeting you for some time. Miss Grant has told me so much about you.'

'Jo Grant?' said the Doctor eagerly. 'She's safe?'

'Safe and well and longing to see you again.' The Controller turned to the guard. 'See that the Doctor is taken at once to the guest suite at Central Control. I'll join you there later, Doctor.'

Deciding to make the most of his new status as an honoured guest the Doctor said simply, 'Thank you,' and allowed himself to be ushered from the cell.

Once the Doctor had gone the Controller said, 'Perhaps we might go to your office, manager?'

The manager was deferential. 'Of course, Controller. This way.'

As they walked along the manager said, 'Excuse my asking, Controller, but who was that man? Why is he so important?' They reached the manager's office and went inside.

'That's no concern of yours,' said the Controller. 'What does concern you is the recent drop in production figures for this work camp. You are becoming too soft. As from next month your work targets will increase by ten per cent.'

'It's impossible, Controller. I can't do it!'

'Shall I replace you with someone who can?' asked the Controller coldly.

'I'm sorry. I'll do the best I can.'

'That's better. We'll consider this a friendly warning, shall we?'

'You're very kind, Controller.'

With a farewell nod, the Controller left the room. The manager waited for a while, looking out across the work compound. Then he closed the door, unlocked a drawer in his desk and produced a tiny communicating device. He spoke into it softly, '*ZV ten to Eagle, do you connect?*'

The crackling voice came back at once: '*This is Eagle, ZV ten. We connect. What is your message?*' (Eagle was the emergency channel of the resistance, manned twenty-four hours a day.)

The manager said, '*Time is short. I think they suspect me. Today a man was captured in the grounds. The Controller himself came to fetch him. I don't know who he is but he's important.*'

'*Do you know why he's important?*'

'*Negative. Check with your source at Central Control. Ask them why—*'

The manager broke off short as his office door was smashed open. An Ogron stood in the doorway, the human security guard behind him. There was no time to conceal the communicator. It's tinny voice said, '*ZV ten, this is Eagle. Do you connect?*'

Deliberately, the manager smashed the communicator to the ground. He waited hopelessly as the hands of the Ogron reached out for him...

In the guest suite at Central Control the first rapturous greetings were over. The Doctor was listening to Jo's account of life in the twenty-second century with more than a little suspicion.

'Honestly, Doctor, it's not so bad. I quite like it

here. Everyone's been very kind… not like those nasty guerillas…'

The Doctor rubbed his chin. 'I'm glad you're being treated so well, Jo. I met some people earlier today who were anything but kind I can assure you.'

The Controller entered in time to hear this remark. 'Now be fair, Doctor. That was a regrettable error, which I put right as soon as I could. You mustn't jump to conclusions.'

The Doctor's manner was distinctly cool. 'Better than jumping to the crack of a whip from some security guard. Tell me, do you run all your factories like that?'

The Controller smiled. 'That isn't just a factory, Doctor. It is a rehabilitation centre for hardened and violent criminals.'

The Doctor was unimpressed. 'Including a large proportion of old men and women?'

'I can assure you,' said the Controller, 'life on this planet has never been more efficiently or more economically organised. People have never been happier or more prosperous.'

The Doctor snapped: 'Then why do you need so many guards around? Don't the people like being so happy and prosperous?'

Jo Grant had been listening to this conversation with increasing dismay. Reproachfully she said, 'You're being a bit unreasonable, Doctor. The Controller only wants to help us.'

'Does he now?' said the Doctor. 'I wonder why?' Turning back to the Controller he said, '*I* find it rather surprising that, with a few rather remarkable exceptions, the human

109

population of this planet seems to lead a life below the level of a dog. It makes me wonder who really rules this Utopia of yours.'

Jo had never seen the Doctor so angry before. The Controller seemed to wither at the sound of the cutting voice. He said haltingly, 'I'm afraid I must leave you. I have work to do. If you'll excuse me, Miss Grant.'

The Controller turned and almost stumbled from the room.

Jo looked after him, worried. 'You shouldn't have spoken to him like that, Doctor. You don't know the whole picture.'

'Neither do you, Jo. Don't you see, Earth has become a slave planet. That man's no more than a sort of superior slave himself. Humans don't rule their own world any longer.'

Jo felt completely baffled. 'Then who does?' she asked.

'The most evil, ruthless life form in the cosmos – the Daleks!' said the Doctor. 'Now just you listen to me.'

He told Jo all he had learned of the true state of affairs in the twenty-second century. Jo was horrified. 'Then why is he being so nice to us?'

'They want to get information. It's an old technique. They've tried the hard treatment. This is the soft. I don't think I want to wait till the hard comes round again.'

Jo shivered. 'Nor do I.'

The Doctor said, 'I got myself captured deliberately. I thought they'd put us together. But now I've found you we need to get away from here!'

Jo lowered her voice. 'There's a guard in the corridor outside.'

The Doctor said softly, 'Don't worry, Jo. I can deal with him.'

The Controller strode down the metal corridors towards the innermost Dalek H.Q. He could still hear the sound of the Doctor's scornful voice. Well, he'd tried to help the man... tried to treat him decently. Now the Daleks could take over. They'd been right all along... it was a waste of time being considerate to such criminals. With thoughts like these the Controller tried to drown the memory of the Doctor's accusing voice. But it was no good. In his heart he knew that everything the Doctor had said was true.

Jo Grant stood in the middle of the guest suite and screamed just as loud as she could: 'Help! Help! Please help me!'

The Ogron guard lumbered through the door and stood looking at her suspiciously. All it could see was the small human girl jumping up and down and screaming. No danger there. It made no attempt to draw its pistol. It stood staring at Jo in amazement as she shrieked, 'Help! Help!'

The Doctor stepped from behind the door and delivered one of his celebrated Venusian karate chops. In theory the Ogron should then have slid quietly to the ground. Unfortunately, it did no such thing. The nervous system of the Ogron race is very resistant to shock, and is also protected by layers of incredibly tough muscle. As a result, the Ogron turned round slowly, and snarled at the Doctor, rather as though he'd stepped on its toe.

Somewhat taken aback the Doctor yelled 'Hai! Hai!' and

delivered three more devastating blows – left hand, right hand, left foot – guaranteed to pulverise any life form in the universe. The only result was that it irritated the Ogron even further. It advanced on the Doctor roaring with rage, and the great hairy paws reached out and grabbed him. Before the Doctor could dodge, the Ogron's hands were locked round his throat. The pressure of the mighty arms sent him slowly to his knees. As consciousness started to slip away the Doctor thought that this was a useful lesson: never underestimate an opponent. Unfortunately, it looked like being the last lesson he would ever learn.

At this point Jo Grant took a hand in things. She jumped on the table, snatched up a full wine bottle and smashed it down as hard as she could on the top of the Ogron's head.

The result was instant and dramatic: the bottle shattered and the Ogron collapsed on top of the Doctor, out cold, wine trickling down its face.

The Doctor wriggled from underneath it, rubbing his throat. 'Thank you, Jo,' he said a little hoarsely.

He remembered the Ogron he had sent crashing into a wall, back in Austerly House. 'Top of the head seems to be their only weak point.' He grinned at Jo. 'Seems a terrible waste of wine, though. Come on, we'd better get moving.'

They moved out into the metal corridor, not running, but walking briskly as though they had a perfect right to go wherever they were going. The people they passed ignored them. In this world of the future, it was safer to mind your own business.

A buzzer sounded, and Jo looked up at the Doctor in alarm. He shook his head, telling her not to worry. Suddenly, the corridor seemed to fill with people all hurrying in one direction. Jo and the Doctor let themselves be carried along with the tide.

Lost in the bustling crowd, they were swept into a big lift which then went down and down for a long time, then out they emerged into a sort of wide entrance hall. Through the big main doors they could see daylight.

The hall was very congested. They followed the crowd out through the doors. A second crowd was trying to get in. 'Shift-changing time,' whispered the Doctor in explanation.

There were Ogron guards at the door, but their only interest seemed to be in keeping the crowd moving with guttural yells, and occasional blows from their whips. They obviously didn't see the crowd as individuals at all, and the different clothes and appearance of the two fugitives seemed to pass unnoticed.

In the Inner H.Q., the Controller was reporting the Doctor's capture to the Black Dalek. He finished his story and waited. Surely this would bring at least a word of praise.

For a moment the Dalek was silent. Then it grated, 'Your description of the Doc-tor does not tally with our files. Repeat.'

Puzzled, the Controller described the tall lean man with the shock of white hair. 'Do you mean this isn't the man?' he asked.

The Dalek said, 'Evidence indicates that the Doc-tor has changed his appearance.' It turned to a Dalek at a control console and said, 'Immediate visual display of suspect!'

The Dalek at the console said, 'I obey.'

It touched a control knob and a screen lit up showing the guest room suite. It was empty except for the Ogron now struggling slowly to its knees...

For a moment the Dalek seemed stunned. Then the Black Dalek screeched: 'Emergency, Emergency... The Doc-tor has escaped! Sound the alarm!'

The Dalek at the console touched another control and a strident alarm began to blare out. The Dalek said, '*The Doctor has escaped. Alert all security units. He must be found and exterminated.*'

The Black Dalek intervened. 'No! We must capture him

alive. We will use the Mind Analysis Machine to discover if this *is* the Doc-tor.'

The Controller shuddered. He had seen captured guerillas after they had been under the Daleks' Mind Analysis apparatus – shambling idiots, with all their intelligence drained from them. Death would be better than that.

The Dalek at the control console spoke into its microphone. '*Cancel previous instructions. The Doc-tor and the girl prisoner are to be captured alive and taken to Mind Analysis area.*'

Jo and the Doctor were crossing a wide, busy compound. Doorways on the far side led to long halls where crowds of people were standing in line to get bowls of grey, unappetising stew. At the end of the compound was a huge, main gate. Through its bars they saw the familiar vista of endless rubble.

The gates were standing slightly open, but there were more Ogron guards on duty there. Unlike those at the doors of the building they were scrutinising keenly all those who went in and out, checking passes and permits. Jo realised that getting out of the building was one thing; getting out of the entire compound was going to be much harder. Which way should they go? They would never get through that main gate. There seemed no point in going back into the main block either. Sooner or later someone would notice them and ask questions.

The Doctor said, 'Look, Jo,' and drew her attention to the main gate. An extraordinary vehicle was jolting across the rubble. It looked like a sort of giant tricycle. It had enormous balloon tyres, and their purpose was obvious: the odd-looking vehicle sped over the rubble as easily as if it were on a paved highway.

The tricycle shot through the gates and into the compound. The Ogron security guard riding it parked it near the gates, jumped off, and clattered up some stairs, carrying some kind of despatch box.

The Doctor looked at the tricycle with interest. 'Useful little vehicle, that,' he murmured. 'Specially developed for crossing all that rubble.'

Jo looked up at him, alarmed by the gleam in his eyes. 'Now, Doctor...' she said, warningly.

A strident alarm began to blare out through the compound. The Doctor yelled, 'Come on, Jo, I think that's for us.' Dragging Jo behind him he ran across the compound to the parked tricycle. He jumped into the driver's seat, and Jo perched up behind him. It took the Doctor only a moment to work out how to use the simple controls. With a roar of power the machine shot through the main gates past the astonished guards, and out across the sea of rubble.

Jo hung tightly to the Doctor as the tricycle sped across the ruined landscape. The little vehicle seemed to be able to cross virtually anything, and they flashed over ruined buildings, occasional bits of road and once even the scrubby and patched remains of a field.

All around was nothing but destruction and desolation, with here and there the jutting towers of the Dalek compounds breaking the horizon. The Doctor pulled up at the top of a little hill, and looked round. Three or four more giant tricycles ridden by Ogrons, were coming from the compound they had just left.

'Can't we outrun them?' asked Jo. 'We've got a good start.'

'We might,' said the Doctor. 'But what about those – and those?' He indicated the other compounds in front of them. From each one was speeding a group of more tricycles.

'We're surrounded!' said Jo anxiously. 'What are we going to do, Doctor?'

'Only one thing we can do,' said the Doctor cheerfully, 'give them a run for their money. Ever wondered how the fox feels, Jo? Hold tight!'

Jo closed her eyes and hung on to the Doctor as hard as she could. The rest of the journey was a nightmare. She saw it only in glimpses as she opened her eyes from time to time, only to close them again hurriedly. The Doctor did incredible things with the giant trike, weaving it in and out of the rubble and the ruins. Jo could have sworn that once they drove up the side of a house and dropped down the other. They zoomed along the tops of walls, leaped over gaps in the ruins, and ploughed through weed-choked ditches. But every time Jo opened her eyes, the circle of their pursuers was drawing in closer.

In a final desperate effort to break through the cordon, the Doctor drove straight off the edge of a small cliff of rubble. The trike shot through the air, and Jo screamed as they landed, bounced, and then crashed into a tangle of broken timbers. There was a jarring impact, and then silence.

The Doctor said gently, 'Open your eyes, Jo. It's all over.'

Jo looked around. Their trike, its handlebars buckled, was jammed in a pile of timbers, wedged far too tightly to move. Around them was a circle of grim-faced Ogrons, guns in hand. The Doctor sighed, 'Well, it was fun while it lasted.'

10

Interrogation by the Daleks

'Rescue him? Why should we risk our lives to rescue the Doctor?' In the guerilla's underground cell, Boaz stared at Moni in disbelief.

Moni's voice was low and urgent. 'I tell you we *must*.'

Anat said, 'Why?'

'When the work camp manager reported the Doctor's capture, he said he was important to the Daleks in some way.' Moni paused. 'He couldn't tell us any more. They must have got him just afterwards. He was executed this morning.'

Anat sighed. The plump, frightened little man had been an old friend of hers. Thanks to his position he had been one of their best agents. But she was used to such losses. They all were. She said, 'Go on.'

'I checked with our contact at Central Control,' Moni continued. 'She's a clerk on the Controller's personal staff.'

'And what did she tell you?' asked Boaz. 'What's so important about one man?'

'It seems the Doctor is a sworn enemy of the Daleks. He's fought and defeated them in the past.'

Anat murmured, 'He did say he'd encountered them before.'

'According to our contact, the Doctor is the one man the Daleks actually fear. Don't you see how important that makes him – to us? He must know a tremendous amount about them. If anyone can help us, he can.'

'Why should he?' asked Anat. 'He's no reason to be grateful to us. We threatened to kill him.'

Moni said, 'That was all a misunderstanding. If we rescue him he'll owe us something. And if he hates the Daleks as much as we do, he's bound to be on our side when we explain.'

Boaz looked dubious. 'An attack on Central Control. It's suicide. A lot of us will be killed even if we succeed.'

'But it will be worth it,' said Moni urgently. 'Look, I need you two because you know the Doctor by sight. Well, what do you say?'

Deep inside the Central H.Q. of the Daleks the Controller looked on impassively as the Doctor was strapped to a long, low table by Ogron guards.

The walls of the little room were lined with strange alien equipment. Dalek scientists monitored control panels. A giant screen filled the whole of the fourth wall.

Once the Doctor was totally immobilised, the Ogrons strapped a silvery helmet over his head. Leads from the helmet ran to the equipment nearest the screen. When all was ready, the Ogrons stepped back. At a nod from the Black Dalek, a Dalek scientist operated some controls. The screen lit up, but only a fuzzy swirling nothingness could be seen.

The Dalek scientist said, 'He is deliberately suppressing

120

his thoughts.'

'More power,' ordered the Black Dalek. The hum of power rose higher and higher. Still the swirling clouds on the screen did not change.

The Black Dalek said, 'You will admit your identity. Who are you?'

As the power rose yet higher a face began to appear on the screen. An old man with a sharp querulous face.

There was a note of triumph in the Black Dalek's voice. 'It is the face of the Doc-tor as we knew him on Skaro. Confess! Confess!'

The Controller saw the Doctor's face distort with the effort of his mental resistance. But it was in vain. Slowly the first face disappeared and a second one took its place. This showed a younger, dark-haired man with a humorous, rather comic face. 'That is also the Doc-tor.' The voice of the Black Dalek rose to a shriek of triumph. 'You *are* the Doc-tor. You are an enemy of the Daleks! Now you are in our power! You will be exterminated! YOU WILL BE EXTERMINATED! YOU WILL BE EXTERMINATED!'

Every Dalek in the room aimed its gun-stick at the Doctor's helpless form.

11

The Raid on Dalek Headquarters

The Black Dalek and his aides gathered round the table to which the Doctor was tied. Their guns were swivelled round to aim at the Doctor. It was obvious that he was to be executed on the spot.

The Controller stepped forward and shouted, 'Stop!' The Daleks swivelled round to face him.

The Black Dalek said, 'Be silent.'

'To kill him now would be a mistake,' said the Controller firmly. 'Don't you see? He can give you valuable help.'

'The Doc-tor is an enemy of the Daleks. How can he help us?'

'He's been in contact with the resistance groups. We know that. Don't you see? He may well be the brain behind them.'

The Black Dalek seemed to consider for a moment. 'You have proof of this?'

'We know that he's been working with them,' said the Controller urgently. 'Why else did he break into the work camp? It must have been to make contact with the manager – a leader of the resistance who has just been executed. Why did he take that risk? Perhaps there is some new plan to attack you.'

The Black Dalek turned back to the Dalek scientist. 'Continue to operate the Mind Analysis Machine. We shall force the truth from his mind.'

The Controller pointed to the Doctor. He was limp and unconscious, his head lolling back against the restraining straps. 'Look at him. You've practically had to kill him just to establish his identity. He'll die before he tells you anything more.'

Again the Black Dalek considered. 'What is your plan?'

'Let *me* interrogate him.'

'Why should you be more successful than the Daleks?'

'I understand how his mind works. I can gain his confidence. Bring pressure on him through the girl.'

There was a moment's silence. Pressing home his advantage the Controller said, 'When I've finished with him we'll have enough information to smash the whole resistance network.'

The Black Dalek swung round to the Ogrons and indicated the Doctor. 'Release him.'

The Ogrons unstrapped the Doctor from the table and dragged him to his feet. The movement seemed to revive the Doctor. Slowly his eyes opened. He looked at the Daleks all round him.

When he spoke his voice was low and determined. 'I've defeated you before. I defeated you on Skaro. I defeated you here on Earth, too.'

The Black Dalek's voice was triumphant. 'The Daleks have discovered the secret of time travel. We invaded again. We have changed the pattern of Earth's history.'

Defiantly, the Doctor said, 'You won't succeed, you know. In the end you will always be defeated.'

'*You* have been defeated, Doc-tor! The Daleks' empire will spread through all planets and all times. No one can withstand the power of the Daleks.'

With the triumphant sound of the Dalek voice ringing in his ears, the Doctor was dragged from the room.

In the guerillas' underground hideout there was a scene of quiet activity. Guns were being cleaned and assembled. Little packs of plastic explosives were being made up. They were getting ready to raid Dalek Headquarters.

Boaz looked round the cellar. It was strange to see new faces in the place that he had shared with Shura and Anat all this while. Another three-man cell had been called in to make up the assault party.

The leader was Mark, a short, stocky man, with hands scarred from years of work in the Dalek mines. It was said that he'd escaped by strangling an Ogron guard. Looking at those broad tough hands, as they assembled a disintegrator gun, Boaz could easily believe it.

Then there was Zando, a round-faced, red-headed lad, with an expression of mild innocence. He looked too young and timid to be a guerilla – a fact which had often saved his life.

Finally, Joab, a shy and timid man who was expert with all forms of explosives. Boaz watched as he rolled a batch of plastic Dalekenium compound into balls the size of a man's fist.

'Steady on,' he protested, as Joab slapped the plastic around like baker's dough. 'Isn't that stuff pretty unstable?'

Joab gave a shy grin. 'Only when it hits a Dalek.' In this form, Dalekenium exploded on impact with a Dalek outer casing.

Boaz crossed to where Moni and Anat were studying a map. Moni was joining their group to replace the missing Shura. He would lead the expedition.

Moni and Anat seemed cheerful and confident as they planned possible routes. Boaz looked at the others in the little cellar. 'You'd think they were planning a day's outing,' he thought bitterly. 'In a few hours' time, some, perhaps all of us, will be dead. And why are we risking our lives? To rescue some mysterious character who'd probably refuse to help us anyway.'

'And to think we had him as our prisoner,' thought Boaz with continuing bitterness. 'If we'd known he was so important, we could have brought him here in the first place.'

Moni folded up the map. 'Well, that's it then. Everybody ready?' There was a murmur of assent. 'We'd better get moving. Time is short.'

Boaz packed up his equipment and followed them from the cellar. Well, Doctor, he thought, you'd better be worth it.

Back in the guest suite the Controller was watching in astonishment as the Doctor made a rapid recovery. When he had been carried from the Mind Analysis Machine the Doctor had seemed broken and exhausted. Now with a little food and wine, and a chance to rest, he was almost his old self again. So much so that he was paying very little attention to the Controller's efforts to convince him that he should co-operate with the Daleks.

'My dear chap,' the Doctor was saying a little impatiently, 'how can I possibly tell you what I don't know myself?'

'But you were in contact with the guerillas,' the Controller persisted.

'Not from choice,' Jo chimed in indignantly. 'They were going to kill him.'

The Controller turned his attack to Jo. 'Can't you see, I'm trying to help him? I've already saved his life.'

'True enough, old chap, and I'm grateful,' said the Doctor, 'but wasn't that just so that you could impress your Dalek masters by getting information out of me?'

The Controller was silent. To be truthful he wasn't sure of his own motives. Certainly that had been part of the reason. But he had also felt a strange reluctance to see the Doctor killed. He tried again.

'Unless you give me information about the resistance – the names of their leaders, the location of their hideouts, their future plans – the Daleks will destroy you.'

The Doctor took another swig of wine and said coolly, 'I don't doubt it.'

The Controller looked curiously at him. 'You value your life so little?'

'On the contrary, I value it enormously. But the Daleks will try to kill me whatever I tell you. They've had it in mind for years.'

'But if you co-operate with them—'

'As *you* co-operate with them?' The Doctor looked at the Controller with a kind of pity. 'You really think it possible to *co-operate* with the Daleks?'

'They can be reasonable,' said the Controller defensively. 'They value my services.'

'They tolerate you,' said the Doctor. 'They allow you to live, as long as you're useful.'

The Controller said angrily, 'I am a senior government official!'

'You're a slave,' said the Doctor simply. 'A slave who has a few privileges in return for helping to oppress his fellow-slaves.'

Suddenly the Controller yelled: 'Be silent!' and Jo saw that he was literally shaking with emotion.

There was a moment's quiet. Then the Controller spoke in a low, hoarse voice.

'You don't understand,' he said. 'No one can understand who doesn't know about those terrible years. Towards the end of the twentieth century a series of devastating wars broke out. There were long periods of nothing but destruction and killing. Nearly seven-eighths of the world's population were wiped out. The rest lived for a long time in holes in the ground, starving, reduced to the level of animals. The entire planet was in ruins.'

Jo and the Doctor were silent, overcome by the horror of the picture he had drawn. Then Jo said softly, 'And that's when the Daleks took over?'

The Controller replied, 'There was no power on Earth to

resist them.'

'So Earth became a giant factory,' said the Doctor. 'All the wealth, all the minerals, carried away to Skaro.'

'But why do they need to do all this?' asked Jo.

The Doctor looked grim. 'Because the Dalek empire is continually expanding. They need a constant flow of raw materials for their war machine. And the planet Earth is particularly rich in minerals.'

The Controller nodded. 'Everyone who is strong enough works in the mines. The rest work in factories, sorting and grading the ore, helping to build weapons for the Daleks. As you say, we're all slaves.' The Controller rubbed his hand over his eyes. It was years since he had allowed himself to think the truth, let alone speak it out aloud.

Jo said, 'How did you come to work for them?'

'Everyone has to work for the Daleks,' said the Controller simply. 'This is better than the mines or the factories.'

'Is it?' said the Doctor. 'Is it really?'

The Controller tried to defend himself. 'I've used my position to help others. I've gained concessions, even saved a few lives.'

'Wouldn't you have helped more by using your skills to lead the fight against the Daleks?' said the Doctor.

The Controller sighed. 'It's hopeless... no one can fight the Daleks.'

'That's not what the guerillas think.'

'A handful of fanatics... most of them killed off already. Believe me... there's nothing they can do to change things.'

*

In a small courtyard at the back of Dalek Headquarters, an iron hatch began to slide open. Moni, Anat, Boaz and the other three guerillas emerged. They looked around them. The courtyard was narrow, dark and windowless. On one side, an archway gave onto a bigger courtyard. On the other, a low ramp ran up to a metal door set into the side of the main building.

The group clustered round Moni, who indicated the metal door. 'This exit is hardly ever used. It's reserved for the Daleks. The door will be locked.'

'We'll open it,' said Joab, fishing out a pack of plastic explosive.

'Up the stairs, along the corridor and we're there,' said Moni. 'It's the nearest exit to the guest suite. Boaz and Anat come with me... the rest of you hold this courtyard, we have to go back the same—' He broke off as an Ogron came into the yard. It reached for its pistol, but immediately Zando tripped it and Mark smashed it over the head with his gun. The Ogron fell without a sound. Moni said, 'Well done.'

Zando grinned. 'We've had a lot of practice.' Anat and Moni moved towards the ramp.

Seconds later it seemed that the little expedition was doomed before it began. Two Ogrons, guns in hand, rushed through the archway from the next courtyard. At the same moment the metal door opened. A Dalek came through it and glided down the ramp, heading straight for Anat. Its gun swung round to cover her.

Zando and Mark and Joab all fired through the little archway at once, blasting the Ogrons out of existence.

At the same moment Boaz grabbed the ball of plastic explosive dropped by Joab. He ran straight at the Dalek menacing Anat and slapped the explosive onto its outer casing. There was a tremendous explosion and Boaz and the Dalek disappeared in a cloud of smoke.

Anat turned blindly to Moni. 'That stuff's *designed* to explode on contact. He must have known.'

'He knew,' said Moni, 'but it doesn't always go off when you throw it. He wasn't taking any chances.' He shook her roughly. 'Now come on! Do you want him to have died for nothing?'

Moni and Anat rushed through the open door and up the stairs. The second group stayed behind as arranged. Zando and Mark kept up a steady fire through the archway, while Joab lobbed balls of plastic explosive.

They were in a good position, but hopelessly outnumbered. They couldn't hope to hold out for very long.

In the guest suite the Controller continued his vain attempt to convince the Doctor that he should furnish information about the guerillas. 'Think what you like of me,' he said wearily, 'but I did save your life. I won't be able to keep you alive unless you give me something to tell the Daleks.'

'I simply don't have any information,' said the Doctor, 'and quite frankly, I wouldn't give it to you if I had.'

Suddenly there came the thump of plastic explosive, and the high-pitched buzz of disintegrator guns.

The Controller leaped up in alarm. He looked round wildly as the sound of firing came nearer. 'Guards!' he shouted 'Guards!' A figure dashed through the doorway, gun in hand. But it wasn't an Ogron guard. It was Anat.

With her was a man they didn't know. He looked at the Controller. 'No use calling for your guards, my friend. They're all dead.'

Anat said, 'Doctor, Jo, are you all right?' Before they could answer, she went on, 'You've no reason to trust me, but please come with us. We need you to help us fight the Daleks. This is Moni, one of our leaders.'

The Doctor said, 'Come on, Jo.' They made towards the door.

Suddenly the Doctor stopped. The other guerilla, Moni, was aiming his gun to shoot down the Controller. 'And as for you...' he was saying.

The Controller stood motionless, waiting. The Doctor said, 'No!'

Moni looked at him in astonishment.

'Killing him won't do any good,' said the Doctor, 'he's not the real enemy.'

Moni said, 'But he's helped them. If you knew of the blood on his hands...'

The Doctor replied, 'They'd always have found someone. Leave him.'

Anat called, 'Moni – let's go.' Reluctantly Moni lowered his gun. Jo, the Doctor and the two guerillas sprinted down the corridor. The Controller stood perfectly still where they had left him. He was stunned, unable to grasp what had happened. He could scarcely believe that he was still alive.

12

Return to Danger

Wrapped in an old blanket Jo Grant huddled close to the wood fire in the brazier. She sipped gratefully at a tin mug full of steaming herbal tea. She looked round the cellar curiously. It was a grim enough place, yet the firelight gave it a homely look. She preferred it to the shining metallic luxury of the Dalek quarters.

The Doctor sat next to her. He too was sipping tea. There was a constant buzz of conversation between the Doctor, Moni and Anat who were all gathered round the fire. Jo knew that three more guerillas had been lost in the rescue. One had been killed fighting a Dalek. Two others had sacrificed themselves to cover their retreat.

Jo's mind drifted back to their escape... everything had happened so quickly. She and the Doctor had followed the guerillas down corridor after corridor and then down a flight of endless steps. Eventually they had emerged into a courtyard. There had been shooting and the thud of explosives, yells and roars and clouds of smoke.

Then they'd all crawled through a little hatchway and along narrow tunnels. Finally they'd crossed what seemed like miles of rubble, stopping to hide from Ogron patrols.

At last they'd ended up here.

Jo tried to concentrate on the conversation going on around her but she kept nodding off. Dimly she was aware that they were talking about Sir Reginald Styles,

The Doctor was saying, 'But how do you know all this? How do you know Styles was responsible?'

'There were still history books,' said Moni impatiently, 'even after the catastrophe. We know.'

Anat took up the story. 'You see Styles only pretended to be working for world peace. Really, he wanted power for himself.'

The Doctor took another swig of his tea. 'So you're saying that this conference he called was a trick?'

'Exactly that,' affirmed Moni. 'He managed to lure all the leading delegates to his house.'

The Doctor said, 'I was told that he was planning a sort of preliminary conference, just before I, er... left Austerly House.'

'Once they were at the house,' said Moni, 'there was a tremendous explosion. The house was completely destroyed. Styles was killed with the others.'

'That wasn't very clever of him,' commented the Doctor.

Moni said, 'Obviously he must have set a bomb. Perhaps he mis-timed the fuse.'

'There were charges and counter-charges,' said Anat, 'and of course the conference was finished. Soon after that war broke out. First with conventional weapons, then with atomic. Thereafter a succession of wars led us to this –' She waved her hand round the cellar.

Moni nodded in agreement. 'And after that the Daleks came and took over what was left.'

The Doctor stared thoughtfully into the fire. 'So you decided to go back in time and intervene in your own history... to kill Styles before he managed to carry out his plan?'

'That's right,' said Moni.

'We stole the plans of time machines from the Daleks. We stole parts and equipment, and managed to build machines of our own.'

Anat joined in. 'At first things didn't go too well. The transference was unstable. People appeared for a while in your time, and then just faded away.'

'That explains the ghost that Styles saw,' said Jo. 'And the man who vanished from the UNIT sick-bay.'

The Doctor nodded. 'Then you three turned up – which is more or less where I came in. By the way, what happened to the other one? That young chap...'

Anat frowned. 'Shura? He simply vanished. We think an Ogron patrol must have got him.'

Moni said, 'Somehow the Daleks learned what we were trying to do. They sent Ogron security guards back into your time to stop us. Shura probably ran into one of them.'

The Doctor looked round the circle of intent faces. 'There's one thing you still haven't told us. Why did you go to so much trouble to rescue us?' He looked quizzically at Anat. 'After all, our first meeting wasn't very friendly.'

Anat said, 'I'm sorry about all that, Doctor. At first we thought you were Styles. When we found out that you weren't, you were just a nuisance. Our mission had to succeed at all costs.'

The Doctor looked across at Moni. 'You still haven't answered my question. Why *did* you rescue us?'

Moni leaned forward. 'We learned later that you were an old enemy of the Daleks, that you'd fought and defeated them before. Surely you'd help us to beat them here?'

The Doctor said, 'If I can – certainly. What do you want me to do?'

Moni said urgently, '*You* can succeed where we failed Doctor. We want you to go back to your own time and kill Styles!'

There was a good deal of bustle and activity around the tunnel near Austerly House. The area was floodlit by spotlights, and by the headlights of army jeeps.

Captain Yates stood before the Brigadier's jeep, with some odds and ends of guerilla equipment. There was food, the shattered booster transmitter, and a stubby looking cylinder with controls set into it.

'We found this stuff in a sort of hiding place, hollowed out beneath some rubble, sir.'

The Brigadier looked at the odds and ends and grunted. 'This all?'

'Yes, sir. No sign of anyone or anything else.'

The Brigadier sighed. He had spent a very long day clearing up after the battle at Austerly House, and carrying out a search of the area. Now he had extended the range of his search as far as the tunnel. Except for this bundle of odds and ends, there had been absolutely no results.

Equally useless had been the Brigadier's efforts to convince the powers-that-be to abandon the idea of a conference at Austerly House. As was often the case in UNIT operations, the Brigadier's reasons were too fantastic to be believed. In addition there was an embarrassing shortage of evidence. The disintegrator guns used by both Ogrons and guerillas destroyed all trace of their victims. Even the bodies of Ogrons killed by bullets had mysteriously faded away. All the Brigadier could produce to support his story were the signs of battle in Styles' study, and the fact that numbers of his own men had vanished.

A sceptical official from the Ministry had looked at Styles' wrecked study and muttered disapprovingly about 'vandalism'. Squads of painters and decorators had worked hard all day to repair the damage, and now even *that* evidence was gone.

The main obstacle though was Styles himself. At present he was in London greeting the other delegates as they arrived. And he was firmly opposed to any change of plan. Arranging the Conference, he said, had been a delicate, almost impossible business. The slightest change in plan might arouse suspicion in the delegates, and send them rushing home again.

The Brigadier could see the old boy's point. And the prize of world peace no doubt justified the risks. But it still left the Brigadier with the problem of trying to protect the Conference.

There was the roar of a motor-bike and a despatch rider

halted by the jeep. The Brigadier took the offered message and tore it open.

'Well, that's it, Mike. No change in plans will be considered. Styles and the other world leaders will arrive first thing tomorrow.' He crumpled up the signal in disgust.

'All we can do is keep searching, Mike. Constant patrols at all times. We'll extend the radius of the search. I want a completely safe area all round the house and grounds. Oh, and keep a heavy guard on this tunnel; it seems to be the centre of things.'

'What about this lot, sir?' asked Captain Yates, indicating his finds from the tunnel. The Brigadier poked the collection with his cane – 'Be careful, sir!' said Yates in alarm. 'The cylinder looks very much like a bomb.'

'Oh, send it all back to UNIT H.Q. The Doctor might like to look at it – *if* we ever see him again.' The Brigadier started his jeep and drove back towards the house. Yates dumped his finds in the back of a UNIT truck. He wondered if the Doctor would ever turn up to examine them. Jo Grant, too, come to that. Mike shook his head wearily and went back to organising the search.

The Brigadier and Captain Yates didn't know it, but two important items were missing from their find in the tunnel. The most important was Shura himself. Then there were the things he was carrying, stuffed into a bulky parcel inside his tunic: a disintegrator pistol. And a Dalekenium bomb.

After the noise and shooting of the Daleks' failed ambush at the tunnel, Shura had drifted off into more uneasy sleep.

138

When he awoke, his condition was worse rather than better. His exhaustion, his wounds, the long spell in the cold damp tunnel had sent him into a high fever. When he awoke he was almost delirious. Only one thought filled his mind: the others had gone, abandoned him! But he himself must complete the mission. He must get back to Austerly House and kill Styles.

Just as darkness began to fall he had emerged from his hiding place, limping along slowly, like a wounded animal. He came out of the tunnel into the cool night air, and stood gasping for a moment. Then he lurched across the fields towards the house. Just as he reached the edge of the field he heard the noise of soldiers coming towards him. He stumbled into a ditch and lay still, covering himself with leaves and bracken. He heard the sound of army vehicles as they parked on the road. Men jumped out, there was a clatter of booted feet, shouted orders. Footsteps thudded by him, within inches of his head.

When it was quiet Shura got to his feet and staggered on leaving the little cluster of vehicles behind him.

Although he didn't realise it, this was Shura's greatest stroke of luck. As the Brigadier's men were spreading outwards from the house, he was moving towards it. Once he'd passed through the line, he and the searchers were moving in opposite directions.

It took him a long time to get into the grounds. He was too weak to climb the wall, so he went round to the main gate and waited. The gate was guarded. Shura waited patiently under cover until a UNIT lorry drove up. While the sentry was checking the driver's pass, Shura somehow scrambled over the tailboard and inside the lorry. It was full of food and drink, cases and cases of it. Sir Reginald and his guests had to be well fed. Shura hastily added a loaf of bread and a bottle to the bundle inside his tunic.

The lorry soon jolted to a halt at the back of the house, and Shura jumped out, slipping into the shadows as the driver came round to unload. The kitchen door stood open, but there were lights on, and he could hear the sound of voices.

Shura moved along the side of the house, looking for a way in. His boots clanged on metal and he looked down. At his feet was a round manhole cover. Shura fished a knife from his pocket and managed to prise it up. Unhesitatingly, he took off his tunic, made a bundle of all his possessions and lowered them through. Then he swung his legs into the dark circle and slid down. He found a foot-hold on something lumpy and shifting. Reaching up again through the hole he dragged the cover back into place. Minutes later a UNIT sentry came round the corner. His boots clanged on the manhole cover just as Shura had it back in place.

Shura fished a light-cell from his pocket and looked around him. He was in a tiny cellar filled with lumpy black stone. He remembered his history. Of course... coal! They used to burn it for fuel...

Shura's incredible luck had served him well again. It was almost as though he was meant to succeed... as though fate was co-operating with him. Austerly House had long ago been converted to oil-fired central heating. But the old coal cellar, and the remnants of the coal, were still there. Nobody ever came to the cellar now.

Shura hollowed out a nest for himself in the coal and settled back. He knocked the top off the wine bottle and took a swig, then stuffed handfuls of bread into his mouth.

Under the influence of the wine and the fever that possessed him he was floating aloof and carefree above the world. Everything was going well. When Styles arrived he would kill him. The mission would be completed. In the pitch blackness of the coal cellar, gun and bomb clutched to his chest, Shura felt calm and happy. All he had to do now was wait.

*

Jo woke up with a start from her doze by the guerillas' fire. Something was happening in the cellar. Voices were raised in excitement. The Doctor was on his feet, pacing about the room.

'Don't you see, man,' he said, 'you're asking me to commit murder! How can I agree to do what you want?'

Anat said, 'We're asking you to kill one man – and to save many more lives.'

'It's still murder,' said the Doctor stubbornly.

'Isn't it justified,' insisted Moni, 'if it would save the human race from the Daleks?'

'Ah, but would it?' said the Doctor, resuming his pacing about. 'Would it?'

Anat looked at him in puzzlement. 'We've told you how it all happened.'

'And suppose your history books got it wrong? Oh, not the basic facts, but their interpretation of them?' He turned to Moni. 'Won't you return us to our own time? Now we know the facts there may be other things we can do to help you.'

'Doctor, please,' said Moni. 'The relationship between our time zone and yours is fixed. A day has gone by here, a day has gone by in your time. Soon it may be too late. Won't you promise to help us? We'll send you back if you'll give us your word to kill Styles.'

'My dear chap,' said the Doctor, 'I'm completely with you as to the ends, but I can't accept your choice of means… and more than that… something feels wrong about the whole idea…'

Jo yawned and stretched. Everyone looked round when

she spoke up. 'Thing that puzzles me is, I just can't believe in Styles as a ruthless mass murderer. I mean he got a bit stroppy, but basically I thought he was quite a nice old boy.' She yawned again.

The Doctor swung round on her enthusiastically. 'That's it, Jo. That's it! Just what was worrying me... that's what I feel, too!' He turned to the guerillas. 'Styles is a *good* man; vain, arrogant, pompous if you like, but underneath it all, good. He really does want world peace, I'll swear it. He couldn't have caused that explosion.'

Anat said, 'Then who did?'

'Let me see that book of yours again,' said the Doctor. Anat passed him the tattered book. Worn almost to pieces by constant handling it was obviously one of the guerillas' greatest treasures. He peered at the faded print and began to read aloud. '*The explosion in the cellar was of such shattering force that it was suspected that a small atomic bomb had been used. But later tests showed no trace of radioactivity. It was charged that the Government had developed some new and deadly "clean" form of atom bomb. This was strongly denied, and no such bomb was ever used in the wars that followed.*'

The Doctor closed the book. An incredible idea was beginning to form in his mind. 'An explosive unknown *at that time,*' he said softly. He looked at Anat. 'And one of you didn't get back from your mission!'

'That's right – Shura. He went to try and contact base. We never saw him again.'

The Doctor said thoughtfully, 'What sort of equipment did you take to the twentieth century?'

Anat said, 'Usual battle gear: disintegrator guns, booster for the sub-temporal radio, food supplies, explosives…'

The Doctor stopped her. 'Explosives?'

'We took two Dalekenium bombs. Just in case…'

'What did they look like?'

'Stubby black cylinders, about so big.' She gestured with her hands. 'Small, but tremendously powerful. We stole them from the Daleks!'

'I don't remember ever seeing you with these bombs,' said the Doctor. 'When you were at the house did you have them with you?'

'Shura hid them for us in the tunnel when we arrived. We didn't have time to pick them up on our way back.'

'Exactly,' said the Doctor. 'Shura hid them in the tunnel where he went to make his attempt to call base. And Dalekenium is a clean explosive. All the power of the atom, but no fall out!'

'Well yes, but…' Anat stared at him in horror. 'No Doctor. It's impossible.'

The Doctor said remorselessly: 'It all fits. An explosive unknown on Earth at the time… Shura, abandoned, wounded perhaps, but determined to carry out his mission… and Styles returning to the house with the other delegates.'

The Doctor looked round the circle of horror-struck faces. 'Don't you see? You want to change history. But you can't. You're part of it, trapped in a temporal paradox. Styles didn't kill all those world leaders. He didn't start the wars that led to the Dalek conquest. *You* did. You did it all yourselves!'

13

The Day of the Daleks

Once again the Controller stood before the High Council of the Daleks.

The Black Dalek, the Golden Dalek and their aides surrounded him, menacing and threatening…

Dully, he listened to the accusing voice of the Golden Dalek. 'You have failed the Daleks. The Doc-tor has escaped.'

'He will be recaptured,' said the Controller. 'I swear it.'

'He must be found and destroyed.'

Wearily the Controller said, 'I am sure he will attempt to return to his own time zone. When he does, and if the guerillas are helping him, they will use the old monorail tunnels. It gives them a fixed reference point near Austerly House in the twentieth century. I can set another ambush – fill the tunnels with guards.'

The Black Dalek said, 'If you fail us you will pay with your life. This is your final chance.'

The Controller turned and walked from the room.

He returned to his office and summoned Zeno, his senior assistant, a sharp-featured, ambitious young man. Briefly, the Controller gave instructions for the ambush. 'I leave the whole thing to you. Don't trouble me with details.'

Puzzled, but happy at a chance to distinguish himself, Zeno returned to his own office. A few moments later his good mood was shattered when he received a summons to appear before the Black Dalek. Hurriedly, he made his way to the inner H.Q., where he waited trembling until the Black Dalek appeared.

Zeno looked at the Dalek in awe and horror. Though he had worked for the Daleks all his life, it was very seldom that he actually saw one. Particularly one of this exalted rank. The Daleks ruled by proxy, and were seldom seen.

The Dalek said, 'We are not satisfied with the loyalty and efficiency of the Controller. It may be necessary for you to replace him!'

Zeno bowed, 'I'm sure that you know best,' he said.

'You will observe him closely during the coming operation. Then you will bring us your report.'

It was still dark when Jo, the Doctor, and the two guerillas made their way across the rubble. Jo was very tired now. She stumbled several times, and the Doctor steadied her with a hand on her arm.

She could remember the hours of argument that followed as the Doctor tried to get the guerillas to accept his theory… their final, reluctant acceptance. Jo hadn't followed all the ins and outs of the argument; all she knew was that at last they were going home, away from this horrible world of Daleks and Ogrons, back to their own time.

Moni halted at the tunnel entrance. 'This is it, Doctor. Anat will take you to a point that is equivalent to the railway tunnel in your own time. Then you'll be transferred. Goodbye and good luck.'

Moni shook hands briefly and turned back. The rest of them plunged on into the darkness. Anat led the way, flashing a little light-cell occasionally to give them their bearings. They plodded on for what seemed an endless time, through the tunnels. At last Anat said, 'We're here!' She shone round her light, and the Doctor recognised the point of his first arrival. Anat produced a time machine. 'It's already set. All you need do is press the operating button.' She, too, shook hands. 'Goodbye, Doctor. I hope you're right about it all. Do what you can for us, won't you?'

She was about to hand over the machine when they were all caught in the beam of a fierce spotlight. A voice said, 'Stay where you are, all of you!'

Ogron guards appeared all round them.

The Controller walked forwards. 'It has ended as I said it would, Doctor. No one can defeat the Daleks. It is madness to oppose them.'

The Doctor walked up to the Controller. He spoke in a low urgent voice.

'I can free this whole world from their rule. I know what happened, how they were able to conquer this planet. I can set Earth's history back onto its proper path. Are you going to stop me?'

In an agonised voice the Controller said, 'If only I could be sure...'

The Doctor said, 'You spoke of the war, the suffering, the starvation... I can stop that from ever happening. *We* can

147

stop it! Will you help me?'

'You saved my life,' said the Controller slowly. 'You could have let them kill me. And now you offer freedom.' He turned to the surrounding Ogrons and said, 'Go! I will deal with these criminals alone! Go I tell you!' Confused, the Ogrons shambled back into the darkness.

The Controller turned back to the Doctor. 'You go, too. Go quickly!'

The Doctor beckoned to Jo. She ran to join him. He looked at Anat. She shook her head. 'I'll stay in my own time, Doctor. Besides, the machine will only transport two.'

Swiftly, the Doctor activated the machine. The glow of the time field surrounded the two figures. Slowly Jo and the Doctor began to fade away.

Zeno came running down the tunnels, armed Ogrons at his heels. He bellowed, 'Stop! Stop them!' But it was already too late – Jo and the Doctor had vanished.

Zeno looked at the Controller. 'You have let them escape. You will pay the penalty for this, Controller.' He turned to Anat, 'And so will you.'

But Anat's gun was already in her hand. She shot out the spotlight and disappeared into the darkness. Zeno made a determined grab for the Controller. To his surprise the Controller was standing quite still: he made no attempt to escape.

Anat ran swiftly through the dark tunnel. She slipped easily through the milling crowds of Ogron guards, shooting out any spotlight that appeared. The Ogrons panicked and fired wildly, killing each other in the process.

Anat came to the point where the Doctor had left the tunnels. The maintenance ladders were an old and familiar escape route. She climbed nimbly upwards and emerged into the fresh air.

She stood for a moment looking over the sea of rubble, the only world she had ever known. There were streaks of light in the east. Dawn was breaking. If the Doctor succeeded it might be a new dawn for all of them. If not, she could always go on fighting. She began to clamber across the rubble, towards the hideout.

After the same mind-twisting voyage through the Time Vortex, Jo and the Doctor found themselves back in the railway tunnel of their twentieth century. 'All right, Jo?' queried the Doctor. She nodded. 'Come on then. There's very little time.'

They ran out of the darkness of the tunnel and cannoned straight into Sergeant Benton who was in charge of the tunnel guard. 'Jo, Doctor!' he yelled. 'Where have you two been?'

'No time for explanations!' snapped the Doctor. 'What's happening at the house?'

Benton looked at his watch. 'Delegates will be arriving for the Conference at any moment. Styles is there already. Wants to make an early start.'

'We may still be in time then,' said the Doctor. 'Lend me a jeep, Sergeant, I've got to get over there right away.'

Benton shrugged. 'I've got to stay here. The Brigadier wants this tunnel guarded. Help yourself, Doc!' He indicated a jeep parked on the road nearby. The Doctor made for it at a run.

Jo said helplessly, 'Hello, and goodbye, Sergeant.' She set off after the Doctor.

For the last time, the Controller of Earth Sector One stood before the Dalek High Council. Somehow he seemed a different man. His shoulders had lost the cowed slump of slavery, and he was free at last from fear, since he had nothing now to lose. He listened quietly while an eager Zeno made his report.

The Black Dalek swung round on the Controller accusingly. 'You will be exterminated! You are a traitor to the Daleks.'

Its gun-stick swung round to cover him. So, too, did the guns of the other Daleks.

The Controller's voice was calm as he said, 'Oh no. I have been a traitor to humanity all my life. But not any more.'

The Black Dalek shrieked with rage, 'You will be EXTERMINATED!'

The Controller smiled. 'Who knows? I may even have helped to exterminate *you*.'

The smile was still on his face when the blast from all the Dalek guns caught him. His body twisted for a moment in an intensity of white light, and then slumped to the ground.

The Black Dalek turned to Zeno as Ogron guards dragged the body of the Controller from the room. 'You have proved yourself worthy to be the new Controller. But be warned… the Daleks expect total loyalty from those who

150

serve them!' Zeno bowed and walked from the room.

The Daleks began to talk amongst themselves in grating metallic voices. It was not so much a conference: since all Daleks think alike it was more a chorus of agreement. The Golden Dalek, the senior, spoke first.

'The Doc-tor is a Time Lord. His intervention may be able to return the course of history to its original path.'

Then the Black Dalek: 'We must follow him to the twentieth century time zone and destroy him.'

'The war amongst the humans must break out,' pronounced the Golden Dalek.

'The Dalek conquest of the planet Earth must not be reversed,' agreed the Black Dalek.

The Daleks left the room to prepare for their expedition. This time they would invade the twentieth century in force.

In spite of the early hour, there was a little crowd of spectators around the gates of Austerly House. They watched with interest as one by one the diplomats arrived in their long, black limousines. There was even a television news team. The commentator was working very hard to make a series of pictures of middle-aged men getting out of cars sound exciting.

'And it is no exaggeration to say that the peace of the world may well depend on what happens here today. On the steps you can see Sir Reginald Styles greeting the Chinese delegate as he steps from his car. The last-minute agreement of the Chinese to attend has given this Conference its greatest chance of success. That agreement is due almost entirely to the efforts of Sir

Reginald himself. Beside Sir Reginald, on the steps, is Brigadier Alastair Lethbridge-Stewart. The Brigadier is, of course, head of the British section of UNIT, the United Nations Intelligence Taskforce, and he is in charge of security at the Conference.'

The commentator paused, racking his brains for something else to say. He was wishing that something, anything, would happen when his wish was suddenly granted. A jeep, driven *very* fast, suddenly shot up the drive and came to a screeching halt at the front steps. A very tall man in rather tattered clothes leaped out, followed by a very small young lady. The tall man rushed up to Styles and the Brigadier, and hustled them inside the building.

The commentator caught a protesting cry of 'Doctor – what do you think you're...' and then the trio disappeared inside the hall.

Inside the Doctor was saying, 'Never mind where I've been. You must evacuate this house at once!'

Styles said furiously, 'Is this man mad?'

'Please, do as he says,' said Jo. 'If you don't, you'll all be blown up!'

'That's right, Brigadier,' said the Doctor. 'Somewhere in this house there's a bomb.'

'Impossible,' the Brigadier said flatly. 'Whole place has been searched.'

'Then search again,' replied the Doctor, 'but clear this building first!'

Styles said, 'I flatly refuse to leave, Brigadier. And I insist this man be removed.'

*

152

In the cellar beneath the house, Shura was priming his Dalekenium bomb. By lifting the lid of his manhole a little earlier he'd been able to hear the noise and bustle of the arrivals. He'd even heard a passing sentry calling, 'Smarten up, there. Old Styles is just arriving.' For Shura that was evidence enough. He'd waited a little longer, finished the last of the bread and wine, and now the bomb was primed. Little figures began to click over on the dial of the bomb. Then they stopped. Shura peered at them muzzily with his light-cell, but they seemed blurred. The timing mechanism had jammed. But it didn't matter. He could easily do without it!

On the road near the tunnel Sergeant Benton leaned against a wall and stretched. He wondered how much longer he'd have to go on guarding this rotten tunnel. Nothing had happened there for ages. He peered into the darkness of the tunnel mouth. Something seemed to be moving.

In the hall of Austerly House time was ticking away and the argument still raged. Styles was adamant, and finally the Doctor gave up. 'Brigadier, get Styles and the rest of them out of this house at once; use force if you have to!'

The Doctor dashed to the wine-cellar door and opened it. He switched on the light. The cellar was empty.

'Cellar, the book said a cellar,' he muttered to himself. Rejoining the group in the hall he said abruptly, 'Sir Reginald… is the wine-cellar the only cellar in the house?'

Sir Reginald looked at him in amazement, convinced by now that the Doctor was quite mad. 'Yes, of course!' he snapped.

The Doctor shook him by the shoulder. 'Think, man, think... there must be another!'

'There's a little coal-cellar by the back kitchen,' said Styles after a moment. 'Never used now, of course.'

As the Doctor was about to rush away the Brigadier's walkie-talkie crackled into life. The Brigadier listened to the agitated voice and said, '*Do your best to hold them, Benton. If you can't, fall back slowly. I'll reinforce you as soon as I can.*'

He turned to the Doctor and said, 'Some kind of attacking force is coming out of the tunnel. Those ape things and something else. Some kind of robots...'

'Daleks,' whispered Jo. 'Daleks and Ogrons!'

The Doctor nodded. 'They're coming to blow up the house and kill Styles – make sure that history goes their way.'

The Brigadier understood none of this, but he was at his best in a military situation. The attack from the tunnel gave him the excuse he needed. He turned to Styles and said crisply, 'You, Sir Reginald, the diplomats and all their staff will evacuate this house at once! Don't argue, man, you can make your protest later. Captain Yates, get them moving!'

Seconds later the television commentator saw the extraordinary sight of a number of very distinguished foreign diplomats being practically thrown into their cars by UNIT troops and driven away at speed. He had no chance to describe this for the viewers however, for minutes later he and his team were being bustled into a jeep and driven away likewise.

In the now rapidly-emptying house the Doctor ran to the little coal-cellar. He burst open the door and saw Shura, lying on the coal, covering him with a pistol. On the coal beside Shura was the stubby little bomb. The Doctor drew a deep breath. 'Shura,' he said quietly. 'You've got to listen to me.'

The invaders from the tunnel advanced remorselessly upon the house. The UNIT troops fought bravely, but could not hold them back. The Ogrons could be killed, though with difficulty. But the Daleks – they seemed invincible. Nothing stopped them as, flanked by their Ogron guards, they glided effortlessly forward. They swept up the drive and were now very close to the house. The Brigadier blazed away from the front steps. Men were being shot down all round him, and he knew that it was only a matter of time...

Jo Grant looked from a window with horror at the advancing Dalek army. Instinctively, she ran to warn the Doctor.

In the coal-cellar doorway, the Doctor, still covered by Shura's gun, was saying persuasively, 'Shura, if you set off that bomb, you'll be sacrificing yourself for nothing. Styles has gone now – he isn't in the house I tell you.'

Shura's hand was resting on the little black plunger. He said dreamily, 'Must kill Styles, must stop the war...'

The Doctor looked at him sadly. Shura's face was gleaming with sweat, his eyes unnaturally bright. The Doctor recognised the signs of high fever. There was little chance of getting through to Shura now.

Jo Grant ran and joined him in the doorway. 'Doctor,

come away! The Daleks are attacking from the tunnel! They're almost in the house…'

She stopped talking as she saw the grim figure of Shura, crouched on the coal, the bomb beside him.

Shura reacted to Jo's voice. 'Daleks? Daleks… here?'

'That's right,' said the Doctor. 'They've come to make sure their version of history isn't changed. Shura, *please*, won't you come with us? We can save you.'

Shura seemed to become suddenly rational. An attacking force of Daleks was something his fevered mind could grasp. 'You two get out of here. Leave them to me. Just let them get into the house…'

Jo said, 'Shura, no! Make him come with us, Doctor.'

'This is Dalekenium,' said Shura. 'The only stuff that will deal with the Daleks – their own bomb!'

'We could rig up a time fuse,' said the Doctor desperately. 'Shura, there must be some other way…'

'The time mechanism is broken,' said Shura. 'Anyway this stuff's too unstable. I'll use the contact plunger. Only way to be sure.' His hand hovered over a black plunger in the side of the bomb. 'Now are you getting out, Doctor? Or do you both want to be here when I press this?'

The Doctor gave him a last look, then said, 'All right, Shura. Come on, Jo!'

The two ran through the empty house to the front steps where the Brigadier, and what was left of his men, were fighting a last desperate rearguard action. Some of the Ogrons had fallen, but most of them were still advancing, the apparently invincible Daleks at their head.

The Doctor ran up to the Brigadier and yelled, 'Fall back! Everyone fall back! Let them into the house. It's the only way.'

The Brigadier shouted, 'You heard the Doctor! Everybody pull back! Re group on the hill behind the house.'

Led by Jo and the Doctor, the Brigadier and his few remaining troops turned and ran. Triumphantly, the Daleks and their Ogron army came on.

From the little hillside behind the house the Doctor and the others watched as a triumphant flood of Ogrons, led by the Black Dalek and the Golden Dalek swept up the drive and swirled into the house. Softly the Doctor muttered, 'Now, Shura, *now!*'

Inside the house the Daleks and their Ogron guards milled about the empty rooms. From his hiding place in the cellar, Shura could hear the angry Dalek voices. 'Where are the delegates?'

'Where is the man, Styles?'

'They must be found and exterminated.'

'The Dalek conquest of the planet Earth must not be reversed.'

'The Daleks will be victorious!'

Shura said softly to himself, 'Oh no, not this time. This time it's going to be different.' With that he pressed the black plunger on the bomb.

From the hillside the Doctor and his group saw the tremendous eruption. It destroyed the house in a single,

savage blast. The noise was shattering. As the black smoke drifted away they saw that the house had completely vanished. No ruins, no debris, just a gaping black hole in the ground...

The Doctor turned to Styles, who was standing nearby. 'Your conference has been saved, Sir Reginald. I hope you make sure it's a success. You still have a choice of futures.'

Styles looked at him wonderingly. 'Don't worry. We all know what will happen if we fail.'

'So do we,' said the Doctor. 'We've seen it, haven't we, Jo?'

Ignoring the puzzled looks from Sir Reginald and the Brigadier, Jo and the Doctor walked down the hill.

14

All Kinds of Futures

'I'm sorry, Doctor,' said Jo obstinately, 'I still don't understand.'

They were walking along the corridor towards the laboratory.

'It's quite simple, Jo. Somehow the Daleks managed to pervert the course of history so they could conquer the Earth. The guerillas tried to change things back, but because they were a part of history, their intervention just repeated the pattern. I was able to intervene and put history back on its proper tracks.'

'I know,' said Jo impatiently, 'because you're a Time Lord. But that still doesn't explain how' – she stopped in amazement as the Doctor flung open the laboratory door. Another Jo Grant was there, looking at her with equal astonishment.

The Doctor said, 'Good grief, yes, of course, I remember now.' He looked at the second Jo Grant. 'Now don't you worry, my dear. I know you're alarmed but—'

To Jo's astonishment a second Doctor came out of the TARDIS. He frowned at them. 'Oh no, what are you doing here?'

Jo heard the Doctor reply. 'Don't worry, I'm not here, that

is… well, in a sense I am here but you're not there… It's a bit complicated to explain.'

'Well, this won't do at all, will it?' said the second Doctor severely. 'Can't have two of us running about.'

'Don't worry, old chap,' said the Doctor. 'It'll all be…'

Suddenly the second Doctor and the second Jo disappeared. Calmly the Doctor walked into the lab and took off his cloak.

'Wait a minute,' said Jo, 'that all happened before. Only they were us and we were them.'

The Doctor smiled. 'Don't worry about it, Jo. I told you time was a very complicated thing.'

The Brigadier entered looking a little shaken. 'I think I've been having hallucinations. For one ghastly moment I thought I saw two of you.'

'Nothing for you to worry about, old chap,' said the Doctor soothingly.

'Ah well,' said the Brigadier. 'Now then, what did I come in for? Oh yes, good news from the Conference. Seeing that explosion seems to have done 'em all good. According to old Styles they're all co-operating beautifully.'

'I'm glad to hear it,' said the Doctor. 'Now if you'll excuse me, I've got work to do.' He opened the door of the TARDIS.

Jo saw that he was about to plunge back into wrestling with the problem of the grounded TARDIS. Before he could disappear she said, 'Doctor!'

The Doctor paused. 'Yes, Jo,' he said patiently.

'That future we saw – with the Daleks ruling the Earth…

is it going to happen, or isn't it?'

'It is, and it isn't,' said the Doctor not very helpfully.

'Oh come on, Doctor,' said the Brigadier, coming to Jo's support. 'What sort of answer is that?'

'I meant exactly what I said,' protested the Doctor. 'First it is – and then it isn't. There are all kinds of futures you know.'

'Futures with Daleks in them?' asked Jo.

The Doctor said, 'It's possible, Jo.'

'But surely those Dalek things were all destroyed?' said the Brigadier.

The Doctor said, 'That was a mere handful… the Daleks exist in many places, and many times. I thought I'd destroyed them once before, but I was wrong.'

The Doctor stood for a moment, gazing into the distance… as if he were looking through time itself, thought Jo, wondering when and where his old enemies would attack again.

The Doctor came out of his daydream and gave her a smile. 'I've just *got* to get the TARDIS working again, Jo,' he said. 'I've got a feeling I'm going to need it.'

With that he disappeared inside the TARDIS and closed the door.

About the Authors

Terrance Dicks

Born in East Ham in London in 1935, Terrance Dicks worked in the advertising industry after leaving university before moving into television as a writer. He worked together with Malcolm Hulke on scripts for *The Avengers* as well as other series before becoming Assistant and later full Script Editor of *Doctor Who* from 1968.

Working closely with friend and series Producer Barry Letts, Dicks worked on the entirety of Third Doctor Jon Pertwee's era of the programme, and returned as a writer – scripting Tom Baker's first story as the Fourth Doctor: 'Robot'. He left *Doctor Who* to work as first Script Editor and then Producer on the BBC's prestigious Classic Serials, and to pursue his writing career on screen and in print. His later scriptwriting credits on *Doctor Who* included the twentieth-anniversary story 'The Five Doctors'.

Terrance Dicks novelised many of the original *Doctor Who* stories for Target, and discovered a liking and talent for prose fiction. He has written extensively for children, creating such memorable series and characters as T.R. Bear and the Baker Street Irregulars, as well as continuing to write original *Doctor Who* novels for BBC Books.

Louis Marks

Louis Marks was born in London in 1928. He worked as a television scriptwriter and script editor all through the 1960s – writing the 1964 *Doctor Who* adventure 'Planet of Giants' for the very first TARDIS crew – before joining the BBC as a script editor in 1970.

It was while at the BBC that Louis Marks wrote the scripts for 'Day of the Daleks' (originally titled 'The Ghost Hunters' and then 'Years of Doom'), later adapting them to add the Daleks as the villains.

Marks wrote two further stories for the series – both featuring the Fourth Doctor: 'Planet of Evil' and 'The Masque of Mandragora'. He went on to become a highly respected television producer working for the BBC on, amongst other productions, *The Lost Boys*, *Play for Today*, *Middlemarch* and *Daniel Deronda*.

Louis Marks died in September 2010.

DOCTOR WHO AND THE DAY OF THE DALEKS
Between the Lines

Terrance Dicks's second *Doctor Who* novelisation was first published simultaneously with Malcolm Hulke's *Doctor Who and the Doomsday Weapon*. It was still early days for Target's Doctor Who range – by this point, the publisher had released only reprints of three 1960s First Doctor stories and adaptations of the first couple of Third Doctor adventures (also by Dicks and Hulke). Like the two books that preceded them, therefore, both *Day of the Daleks* and *The Doomsday Weapon* needed to work just as well as introductions to the series for new readers as they did for longer-standing fans. The TV serials on which they were based were by then two or three years old, and *Doctor Who* was constantly attracting new young viewers, just as it has been in the 2000s.

With this in mind, Terrance Dicks greatly expanded on events seen in 'Day of the Daleks' when it was broadcast in January 1972, drawing on Louis Marks's original scripts and adding his own inventions. The whole of Chapter 1 is new to the novel. The TV story offers only glimpses of twenty-second-century Earth under Dalek rule in its first two episodes, but Dicks's scene setting here paints a much fuller picture, even showing Ogrons chatting around campfires. This future Earth, we later discover, is one still suffering the after effects of an atomic war, with low levels of radiation still in evidence; Louis Marks's episodes said only that there had been 'a series of wars'. Dicks goes further still with his portrayal of the effects of the Dalek presence, revealing modern constructions that can only be described as 'Daleky'. The Daleks' rubble-clearing labour camp is also shown in more detail in Chapter 8, with the Doctor even compelled to intervene before his capture. In Chapter 9, he tells the Controller that he, too, is just a slave to the Daleks, rather than 'a traitor … a quisling', as on TV, and the novel's Controller no longer comes from a family of quislings.

The other major addition is the pay-off to Chapter 2's scene showing the Doctor and Jo encountering their future selves, with the whole of Chapter 14 presenting events (and explanations, of sorts) not seen on TV. The scene was in fact scripted and recorded but was cut before broadcast to stop Episode 4 overrunning. The first half of the Doctor's final line in that deleted scene is not incorporated into the book: 'I thought I'd destroyed [the Daleks] once before, but I was wrong. I must get the TARDIS working again, Jo. I think I'm going to need it.' Another cut scene – also absent from the novel – comes early in Episode 4, with the Doctor recalling that he had orchestrated a civil war on Skaro that had supposedly destroyed the Daleks ('The Evil of the Daleks', 1967); the Daleks reveal that the rebellion was unsuccessful.

These post-civil war Daleks, like the Time Lords, now have a High Council. According to Dicks's novel, this council rules planet Earth, but it is not mentioned on screen and seems to be distinct from the Supreme Council referred to in the subsequent story 'Planet of the Daleks'. The Daleks in TV's 'Day of the Daleks' are led by a gold Dalek, called 'Chief Dalek' in the *Radio Times* listings, but 'Golden Dalek' in the scripts and novelisation. On screen, the Golden Dalek is part of the first reveal of the Daleks at the end of Episode 1, but Dicks holds him back until halfway through the novel; until Chapter 8, a Black Dalek seems to be running things. A Black Dalek was first seen in 'The Dalek Invasion of Earth' (1964), and was the supreme controller of the Daleks' original conquest of twenty-second-century Earth. The Black Daleks continued to appear throughout the 1960s, and were revealed to be a distinct rank ('Black Dalek leaders') in 'The Evil of the Daleks', which proved to be their final appearance. For 'Day of the Daleks', the non-golden Daleks are painted a dark metallic grey and black, variations of which would dominate for their next few TV appearances. By the time a black Dalek was seen on screen again, in the 1980s, it was calling itself the Supreme Dalek.

The novel has the Doctor working on his repairs inside the TARDIS – in Episode One, the control console has somehow been extracted from the police box, as it had been in the stories 'The Ambassadors of Death' and 'Inferno'. This allows a moment in Chapter 2, with smoke billowing from the police box doors as the Doctor bursts out, which is a familiar comic trope from the Third Doctor's stories. (He's also 'cursing fluently in an obscure Martian dialect', which is a particular talent of the Doctor's, but only in print.)

As on screen, Sir Reginald Styles is a fairly unsympathetic character, but he also gains some unexpected experience of armed combat and actually fights back when first attacked in Chapter 2. The introduction of a UNIT squaddie yearning for London's pavements also allows a glimpse of an unscreened briefing by the Brigadier. The Brigadier's 'phone call from 'the Minister' is expanded here as well, not least in noting that the Brigadier had been intending to ignore the report from Austerly House – perhaps a little odd, given that he already has UNIT sentries stationed there (unlike on TV) and has some experience of the odd and the unexplained…

Sergeant Benton and his UNIT troops also get their first sighting of the Ogrons in Chapter 2, much earlier than in the TV story. Neither the Doctor nor the Brigadier seems especially interested, though, preferring to follow the scripts in concentrating on the possibility of ghosts. More sensibly, the unconscious guerilla being guarded by Benton does his vanishing act from the UNIT sick-bay, rather than from an ambulance that seems, on TV, to take several hours to reach its destination.

The Doctor's laboratory – in this story only – contains a fortuitously placed firing range for testing mysterious future weaponry; Terrance Dicks replaces that here with a home-made Guy Fawkes dummy courtesy of Jo Grant, who even lipsticks a happy face onto it.

The guerillas' arrival in the twentieth century is extended to include much more unpacking of equipment and discussion of their mission. When they imprison the Doctor and Jo in the cellar in Chapter 5, we are told that 'he managed to pull her gag away with his teeth'. Episode Two shows Jo wriggling free on her own, which was perhaps a little easier to stage.

Once she reaches the twenty-second century, Jo Grant is even more forthcoming about the Doctor than she is in the TV story. She even tells the Controller all about UNIT, despite her luxurious meal apparently being rather less fabulous than the one she enjoys on screen.

In print, the motorised trikes are rather speedier and enormously more capable than their televison counterparts – there was not even the smallest hint on screen that the Doctor might manage to drive one up and down the sides of a house. Dicks also drops in a clear nod to Jon Pertwee's obsessive enthusiasm for all forms of transport around here, with Jo noting with alarm the gleam in the Doctor's eyes when he first spots a trike.

On TV, Shura's disappearance is rather overlooked until the Doctor asks about him in Episode 4. Here, Dicks follows his progress more carefully. He also makes it clear that Boaz's death is a deliberate act of self-sacrifice, which is not specified on screen. In fact, the twenty-second-century conflict between the guerillas and the Ogrons leading up to the Doctor being rescued in Chapter 11 is extended considerably. There's also more detail in Chapter 13 as the Doctor escapes, showing Anat fleeing the tunnel and confused Ogrons killing each other.

There are smaller differences, too. TV's 'Central Zone' is 'Earth Sector One' in the novel. The resistance leader Monia is now Moni. Auderly, Styles' residence, meanwhile, is renamed Austerly House, apparently to avoid confusion with a real-life location. Several minor characters are given names, including the three guerillas Mark, Zando and Joab, whose screen life had been too short for them to merit a christening. (Mark is mentioned briefly on screen as one of those who has given his life to rescue the Doctor.) And the Controller's eventual successor is now known as Zeno, not just 'Senior Guard'.

One word is used in both novel and TV story: Dalekenium, the name given to the guerillas' explosives, stolen from the Daleks, although it's spelt 'Dalekanium' in Louis Marks's scripts. In an earlier story ('The Dalek Invasion of Earth', 1964) and a later story ('Daleks in Manhattan', 2007), however, Dalekenium is the metal used in Dalek casings.

Doctor Who and the Day of the Daleks was originally published in April 1974, when Jon Pertwee's Doctor was facing 'The Monster of Peladon' on Saturday evenings on BBC One; it was just a month since the Daleks had last been seen on TV, in 'Death to the Daleks'. The cover and internal illustrations were by Chris Achilleos. This new edition re-presents that original 1974 publication. A few minor errors or inconsistencies have been corrected, but no attempt has been made to update or modernise the text – this is *Doctor Who and the Day of the Daleks* as originally written and published.

This means that the novel retains certain stylistic and editorial practices that were current in 1975 (when the book was written and prepared for publication) but which have since adapted or changed. Most obviously, measurements are mostly given in the then-standard imperial system of weights and measures: a yard is equivalent to 0.9144 metres; three feet make a yard, and a foot is 30 centimetres; twelve inches make a foot, and an inch is 25.4 millimetres.

Like its televised source, the novelisation makes much of 'the international situation'. Possible conflict between America and Russia and potential intervention by China was a real and constant worry in the 1970s, with the end of the cold war still well over a decade away. Britain's role as would-be peacemaker or intermediary is a feature of several *Doctor Who* stories of that time, such as 'The Mind of Evil' and 'Robot'.

Less often a major element of the series, though, was such a firm focus on time travel and its complexities – perhaps surprisingly to fans of Matt Smith's Doctor. This is one of just a handful of stories from the show's original 1963–1989 run that goes anywhere near notions of temporal paradox. 'Day of the Daleks' introduces something called the 'Blinovitch Limitation Effect', which Terrance Dicks helpfully explains in this novelisation: 'The relationship between our time zone and yours is fixed. A day has gone by here, a day has gone by in your time.' In the years that followed, this would become an important – and sometimes remarkably flexible – element of the rules of time travel…

Here are details of other exciting Doctor Who *titles from BBC Books:*

DOCTOR WHO AND THE DALEKS
David Whitaker   £4.99
ISBN 978 1 849 90195 6   **A First Doctor adventure**

With a new introduction by **NEIL GAIMAN**

'The voice was all on one level, without any expression at all, a dull monotone that still managed to convey a terrible sense of evil...'

The mysterious Doctor and his granddaughter Susan are joined by unwilling adventurers Ian Chesterton and Barbara Wright in an epic struggle for survival on an alien planet.

In a vast metal city they discover the survivors of a terrible nuclear war – the Daleks. Held captive in the deepest levels of the city, can the Doctor and his new companions stop the Daleks' plan to totally exterminate their mortal enemies, the peace-loving Thals? More importantly, even if they can escape from the Daleks, will Ian and Barbara ever see their home planet Earth again?

This novel is based on the second Doctor Who *story, which was originally broadcast from 21 December 1963 to 1 February 1964. This was the first ever* Doctor Who *novel, first published in 1964.*

DOCTOR WHO AND THE CRUSADERS
David Whitaker   £4.99
ISBN 978 1 849 90190 1   **A First Doctor adventure**

With a new introduction by **CHARLIE HIGSON**

*'I admire bravery, sir. And bravery and courage are clearly in
you in full measure. Unfortunately, you have no brains at all. I
despise fools.'*

Arriving in the Holy Land in the middle of the Third
Crusade, the Doctor and his companions run straight
into trouble. The Doctor and Vicki befriend Richard the
Lionheart, but must survive the cut-throat politics of the
English court. Even with the king on their side, they find
they have made powerful enemies.

Looking for Barbara, Ian is ambushed – staked out in the
sand and daubed with honey so that the ants will eat him.
With Ian unable to help, Barbara is captured by the cruel
warlord El Akir. Even if Ian escapes and rescues her, will
they ever see the Doctor, Vicki and the TARDIS again?

This novel is based on a Doctor Who *story which was originally
broadcast from 27 March to 17 April 1965, featuring the First
Doctor as played by William Hartnell, and his companions Ian,
Barbara and Vicki.*

DOCTOR WHO AND THE TENTH PLANET
Gerry Davis   £4.99
ISBN 978 1 849 90474 2   **A First Doctor adventure**

With a new introduction by **TOM MᴀᴄRAE**

'We were exactly like you once. Then our cybernetic scientists realised that our race was weakening. Our scientists and doctors invented spare parts for our bodies until we could be almost completely replaced.'

The TARDIS brings the Doctor and his friends to a space tracking base in the Antarctic – and straight into trouble. A space mission is going badly wrong, and a new planet has appeared in the sky.

Mondas, ancient fabled twin planet of Earth, has returned. Soon its inhabitants arrive. But while they used to be just like the humans of Earth, now they are very different. Devoid of emotions, their bodies replaced with plastic and steel, the Cybermen are here.

Humanity needs all the help it can get, but the one man who seems to know what's going on is terminally ill. As the Cybermen take over, the Doctor is dying…

This novel is based on the final story to feature the First Doctor, which was originally broadcast from 8 to 29 October 1966, featuring the First Doctor as played by William Hartnell in his very last adventure, and his companions Ben and Polly. This was the first Doctor Who *story to feature the Cybermen.*

DOCTOR WHO AND THE CYBERMEN
Gerry Davis   £4.99
ISBN 978 1 849 90191 8   A Second Doctor adventure

With a new introduction by GARETH ROBERTS

*'There are some corners of the universe which have bred the most
terrible things. Things which are against everything we have
ever believed in. They must be fought. To the death.'*

In 2070, the Earth's weather is controlled from a base on the
moon. But when the Doctor and his friends arrive, all is not
well. They discover unexplained drops of air pressure, minor
problems with the weather control systems, and an outbreak
of a mysterious plague.

With Jamie injured, and members of the crew going
missing, the Doctor realises that the moonbase is under
attack. Some malevolent force is infecting the crew and
sabotaging the systems as a prelude to an invasion of Earth.
And the Doctor thinks he knows who is behind it: the
Cybermen.

This novel is based on 'The Moonbase', a Doctor Who *story which
was originally broadcast from 11 February to 4 March 1967,
featuring the Second Doctor as played by Patrick Troughton, and
his companions Polly, Ben and Jamie.*

DOCTOR WHO AND THE ABOMINABLE SNOWMEN

Terrance Dicks £4.99

ISBN 978 1 849 90192 5   **A Second Doctor adventure**

With a new introduction by **STEPHEN BAXTER**

'Light flooded into the tunnel, silhouetting the enormous shaggy figure in the cave mouth. With a blood-curdling roar, claws outstretched, it bore down on Jamie.'

The Doctor has been to Det-Sen Monastery before, and expects the welcome of a lifetime. But the monastery is a very different place from when the Doctor last came. Fearing an attack at any moment by the legendary Yeti, the monks are prepared to defend themselves, and see the Doctor as a threat.

The Doctor and his friends join forces with Travers, an English explorer out to prove the existence of the elusive abominable snowmen. But they soon discover that these Yeti are not the timid animals that Travers seeks. They are the unstoppable servants of an alien Intelligence.

This novel is based on a Doctor Who *story which was originally broadcast from 30 September to 4 November 1967, featuring the Second Doctor as played by Patrick Troughton, and his companions Jamie and Victoria.*

DOCTOR WHO AND THE ICE WARRIORS
Brian Hayles   £4.99
ISBN 978 1 849 90477 3   ·   A Second Doctor adventure

With a new introduction by MARK GATISS

Varga struck the fractured ice with his great fist. He faced his comrades boldly and barked a command at their lifeless forms: 'Awake from the dead!'

The world is in the grip of a second Ice Age. Despite a coordinated global effort, the glaciers still advance. But they are not the only threat to the planet.

Buried deep in the ice, scientists at Britannicus Base have discovered an ancient warrior. But this is no simple archaeological find. What they have found is the commander of a spaceship that crashed into the glacier thousands of years ago. Thawed from the ice, and knowing their home planet Mars is now a dead world, the Ice Warriors decide to make Earth their own...

Can the Doctor and his friends overcome the warlike Martians and halt the advance of the glaciers?

This novel is based on a Doctor Who *story which was originally broadcast from 11 November to 16 December 1967, featuring the Second Doctor as played by Patrick Troughton, and his companions Jamie and Victoria.*

DOCTOR WHO AND THE AUTON INVASION
Terrance Dicks   £4.99
ISBN 978 1 849 90193 2   **A Third Doctor adventure**

With a new introduction by **RUSSELL T DAVIES**

'Here at UNIT we deal with the odd – the unexplained. We're prepared to tackle anything on Earth. Or even from beyond the Earth, if necessary.'

Put on trial by the Time Lords, and found guilty of interfering in the affairs of other worlds, the Doctor is exiled to Earth in the 20th century, his appearance once again changed. His arrival coincides with a meteorite shower. But these are no ordinary meteorites.

The Nestene Consciousness has begun its first attempt to invade Earth using killer Autons and deadly shop window dummies. Only the Doctor and UNIT can stop the attack. But the Doctor is recovering in hospital, and his old friend the Brigadier doesn't even recognise him. Can the Doctor recover and win UNIT's trust before the invasion begins?

This novel is based on 'Spearhead from Space', a Doctor Who story which was originally broadcast from 3 to 24 January 1970, featuring the Third Doctor as played by Jon Pertwee, with his companion Liz Shaw and the UNIT organisation commanded by Brigadier Lethbridge-Stewart.

DOCTOR WHO AND THE CAVE MONSTERS

Malcolm Hulke £4.99

ISBN 978 1 849 90194 9 A Third Doctor adventure

With a new introduction by TERRANCE DICKS

'Okdel looked across the valley to see the tip of the sun as it sank below the horizon. It was the last time he was to see the sun for a hundred million years.'

UNIT are called in to investigate security at a secret research centre buried under Wenley Moor. Unknown to the Doctor and his colleagues, the work at the centre has woken a group of Silurians – intelligent reptiles that used to be the dominant life form on Earth in prehistoric times.

Now they have woken, the Silurians are appalled to find 'their' planet populated by upstart apes. The Doctor hopes to negotiate a peace deal, but there are those on both sides who cannot bear the thought of humans and Silurians living together. As UNIT soldiers enter the cave systems, and the Silurians unleash a deadly plague that could wipe out the human race, the battle for planet Earth begins.

This novel is based on 'The Silurians', a Doctor Who *story which was originally broadcast from 31 January to 14 March 1970, featuring the Third Doctor as played by Jon Pertwee, with his companion Liz Shaw and the UNIT organisation commanded by Brigadier Lethbridge-Stewart.*